GOD'S
BEDFELLOWS

GOD'S BEDFELLOWS

stories by
David Carpenter

M&S

CANADIAN CATALOGUING IN PUBLICATION DATA

Carpenter, David, 1941-
  God's bedfellows

ISBN 0-7710-1917-3

I. Title.

PS8555.A76G62 1988   C813'.54   C88-093237-6
PR9199.3.C35G62 1988

Printed and bound in Canada by Friesen Printers

Design by: T.M. Craan

The publisher thanks the Ontario Arts Council for its support.

McClelland and Stewart
The Canadian Publishers
481 University Avenue
Toronto M5G 2E9

This book is for my mother, Marjorie Carpenter, the neighbourhood poet for many years. She was the first one to convince me that a boy could do worse than read good books.

Contents

Crossing the Line

1

I used to tell this story during my drinking days down at the Athabasca. It was a good test of people's sobriety. The moderate drinkers would give me that Oh-sure-Barney look, and the drunks would grow wide-eyed with belief and make me feel for a while like a prophet. I've told two people this story when I was completely sober: my wife Molly, and my younger brother Darryl. Molly took the diplomatic approach and said there were certainly parts of it that rang true, but Darryl looked at me as if to say, So that's where all that reading and education got you. "You were always the one with the imagination," he said later. Spiritless little prig.

I too have had problems with believing things. It's a family trait. Before my mother met my father, she believed in salvation through Jesus Christ and he believed in oblivion through Johnnie Walker. She agreed to lay off the church if he agreed to lay off the bottle and they got married in 1944. I was the fruit of their brief armistice. I've tried Mom's church and Dad's boozing, and as far as I'm concerned neither one inspires belief in anything worthwhile. I'm on the wagon from both, and Molly says that's just fine with her.

So I've decided to write this thing down and send it somewhere, a magazine maybe, the kind that will print things that most magazines won't; the kind that will print a story in which a guy can call his brother a prig, for instance. And if a magazine or newspaper won't take it I'll send it to the Jasper archives and let someone else live with this thing for a while.

It began with the death of Annette Muskwa in a TB hospital around 1948. Her husband, Noel Muskwa, was left without anyone to take care of their youngest child, so Nokom (everyone's name for Annette's mother) came and lived with them. The child was Delphine Muskwa, an afterthought you might say. She was my only real playmate until I was eight or nine years old. She had long black hair, a mouth that reminded me of cartoon frogs, and when she smiled, her eyes disappeared. Delphine Muskwa. Sometimes just saying her name makes me feel sentimental.

Delphine's dad Noel was a trapper and a hunter. Due to pressure from Annette, and because of his own love of solitude, Noel always kept his distance from the reservation. Today we would probably call Noel and his family non-status or non-treaty, but in those days Father called them bush people, and around there that explained everything. Noel was what my mother called "a difficult man." No one could ever get him to do anything he didn't feel like doing.

We must have been extremely dependent on them: Father on Noel because (in spite of his intractability) he knew so much about the bush, he was handy, and liked my father; Mother on Annette for several years before her death, because she was someone to visit with; I on Delphine because she was good to play with; and all of us on Nokom because she knew things about sickness and babies and the like.

Every summer after the Indian Days rodeo Noel's people would pay him a visit. These were reservation Indians (what my grandmother Sharples called "real red Indians"): uncles, aunts, Noel's older children, and dozens of his children's children, and some very old people who spoke Cree with a little sprinkling of French. They came in wagons, some of the young men on ponies. All hell broke loose in a nice sort of way for me and in a fretful sort of way for my parents. Delphine would grab hold of me and we'd run off with all the other kids and go fishing or play games. Once I'd been given the okay from Delphine, I was accepted; that's all there was to it. My parents would worry that we'd run into a bear, which we sometimes did on the upper meadow, but nothing ever happened, except later of course, and that's something I'll get to.

The Muskwa men were a peace-loving lot, but one or two of them would sometimes get drunk. That meant climbing my father's tower, which usually meant falling off, which in turn meant the clown in question would have to get taken to town because Nokom, for all her medicinal know-how, was never much good at setting bones. Once one of the uncles, Clayton Muskwa, an obnoxious fellow drunk or sober, took Father's half-ton and drove it into the Muskwa's backhouse. Trying to pull out, he high-centred the truck on a stump. It took a team of horses to pull it off and my father lost his muffler. He got awful mad.

He must have made a compromise with himself. Like most reformed drinkers, he disapproved of drinking and carrying on, but he knew how much we all depended on the Muskwas; so he tolerated their occasional summer excesses and counted the days till the uncles and their families would pack up the wagons and head back down the trail. Which they did whenever Nokom had had enough of what she called "Injun's people." She always called her son-in-law "Injun." I'm not sure why. Maybe she associated Noel with his former reservation. The reservation was anathema to her. After Annette's death, Noel used to swear he'd go back to it, but he never did go back. He just missed his wife, I think.

Trapping and hunting inside Jasper Park were and still are illegal, so Noel did his trapping and hunting just outside the park boundary. He claimed the boundary was exactly one quarter of a mile from the east end of his and Dad's corral. He may have been telling the truth here, because when the school district was surveyed Noel seemed to know to within a few yards where the line came. I think he had a sixth sense for that sort of thing.

Before their kids grew up and left them, in fact before Delphine was born, Noel and Annette tried living in a shack at the edge of town. His idea then was to live near town but not in it, because if he was within the town limits his children would have to go to the residential school. He absolutely refused to let his kids go to any school, least of all the one where he'd lose them for most of the year.

When the school district was formed, he built another shack in the bush. He claimed this new shack was just a bit outside the new line. He eyeballed it, as they say. When a school official came to his door and said the kids had to obey the law and go to school, he simply pointed to where the line was and said as long as he was outside that line, no child of his would ever set foot in that damned school. So they surveyed the line, putting in stakes, and sure enough, Noel's cabin was outside by several yards.

The town grew. With its collective eye on more tax dollars, the school district expanded. Once more Noel and family abandoned their shack and threw up a cabin back in the bush. Once more the authorities drove out to claim the children and once more they discovered that Noel's new cabin was just a few feet on the other side of the boundary.

He told them what they could do with their "residentzel scole." The first year our cabins sat side by side on Celestine Lake, Noel had moved his family half a dozen times. This time he was so far from the school line he could feel safe for years. He and the last of his family lived winter and summer in that last cabin of theirs. It always smelled richly of hides, moose meat, dogs, bannock, berries and tobacco, many of the things I couldn't smell in my own home.

Around the time I was born my father manned the forestry tower every spring and summer at Celestine Lake, which is just inside the eastern boundary of Jasper Park among the hoodoos and gravelly ridges too high to be called hills and too low to be called mountains. Nokom attended at my birth. I was supposed to be born in the Jasper hospital but I came several weeks early, and old Nokom was there. My mother preferred her to the doctor in town who, according to Mother, was a whisky-soaked old coot. She liked to stress that fact in Father's presence, which was always good for a tirade from him on the subject of Bible thumpers.

For half a dozen years or so Delphine was the only permanent kid up there my age. My parents would tease me and call her my girlfriend, but I think they were grateful for Delphine because she and her many cousins gave me something to do and somewhere to go in those endlessly long days from June to September when time seemed to crawl along like a garden slug.

Comic books were the key. We acted them out even when there was just the two of us. We got to be animals and other people. Absolutely the best one for acting things out was *Tarzan*. If you got to be Tarzan himself, you could give great war whoops and swing on the rope that always hung from the Douglas fir in front of the corral. Or if you were Tantor, you got to lumber through the forest on your hands and knees with Tarzan or Boy or Jane on your back and everyone ran from you. They had to. You were the elephant and that was the game. And if you were one of the apes or one of the natives you got to yell things like, *Kree-gah Gomangani! Bundolo, kill!*

Delphine did animals real well. When she became Tantor and crashed through the trees, you never doubted that she was Tantor. And when she was a monkey (I taught her monkeys; I'd seen one at the fair in Edson) she hopped around all hunched over, gibbering, arms dangling. By God she was a monkey. And when she did a bear, she'd walk on her hind legs, beat the air with her front paws, scrunch up her face, and look fierce. Boy, let me tell you, she was a bear. She could scare me sometimes.

I have a photograph of her and me at Celestine Lake. I think Mother took it. We're holding hands and squinting at the person with the camera. We're both eight or nine years old, skinny, and very brown. My smile is a bit shy; Delphine's is smug, like she has a secret and she's not telling.

Two or three times between the first of May and the Labour Day weekend, we had to drive to town. My father would go about his business at the warden's office, my mother would get provisions in the truck, and Delphine and I would go down to the CN station. It had to be timed just right. The bears would arrive as the train came in and leave minutes after it left. Their timing was never off.

When you heard the chugging of the Edmonton train just after ten a.m., all you needed to do was look west on Connaught Drive and there they'd be, ambling toward you: mamas and cubs, uncles and aunts, old boars with chewed-up ears, cinnamon bears, dark brown ones, but mostly black with a white star on the chest, and mostly ragged looking, like gypsies. They'd come down the main street in twos and threes, slowly at first, stop and sway their heads smelling the air, listening like old blind men. Then the older ones would pick up the pace, look a bit bolder, the cubs would tussle a bit, get behind, scamper back; until finally they'd all be gathered on the grass beneath the totem pole where the passengers debarked. The bears were never pushy about their panhandling. They just waited there pretending not to be hungry and stayed out of the redcaps' way until the show began.

After the shock wore off from seeing this army of bears out there, the tourists would grab their cameras and any junk food they could get their hands on. They'd pay the redcaps large sums of money to have their pictures taken with the bears. Occasionally a man would try to find a docile one and place his hat on the bear or induce it to stand up so he could put his arm around the bear or clap it on the back. These games of course proved worrisome for the park wardens because sometimes a tourist would pick the wrong bear to get familiar with. This must have been before the time when fear of lawsuits governed all human behaviour, because (knowing bears were good for the tourist business) all Thurmon Butters the superintendent did was put up a snow fence on the grassy area with a ten-foot opening for the bears. No people were allowed inside the fenced area. The tourists would gather on one side of the fence; the bears, on their hind legs, would rest their front paws on top of the fence and sort of sway back and forth with the give and take of it. These fences are insidious things. They have their own logic, like Slinkies.

Word got around that the best way to feed a bear was to put your hands on the fence and gently lean towards the animal. The tourist didn't want the bear falling onto his side of the fence, and he sure as hell didn't want to fall onto the bear's side, so both bear and tourist tended to respect that fence. Coca-Cola seemed to be the preference among the younger bears. The tourist would invert a six-cent bottle of Coke, baby bottle fashion, into the bear's mouth and watch the bear slobber Coke till it was all gone. It was considered particularly touching if the young bear in question would rest its paws on the wrist of the tourist long enough for the other tourists to say "awww" and click their shutters.

Up on the alpine meadow north of Celestine we had *real* bears, grizzlies. They were big, and they weren't garbage bears. Once in a while a family of these grizzlies would amble down from the high country into our meadow. I have very good eyes, so I usually spotted them before Delphine did. We'd watch them for hours, downwind of course, and in the trees, so we could scamper up one if they got our scent and charged. But none ever charged us.

I can still see those bears. The sun brought out the pale gold in their fur and the wind made dark ripples through it. Their humps were like dry grassy hills. I remember grizzlies not as *Ursus horribilis*, killers or brutes, but creatures of golden light, otherworldly, big-bellied like Sumo wrestlers.

One morning I came early to breakfast. Mom looked worried. I think that's when she was pregnant with my brother. Dad was talking on the radio, yelling rather, and swearing. With him that was always a bad sign.

"Fine, Thurmon, I'll just abandon my tower and hightail it down there like I've got nothing better to do –" And, "Fine, Thurmon, I'll just toady to the tourists. That's what we're paid to do, right? Toady to the goddam tourists?"

Like I said, Thurmon Butters was the superintendent. He was a big man with a soft paunch. He always wore sunglasses and his hair combed straight back like a gangster's, and he always had a toothpick in his mouth. His best friend was a sergeant in the Mounties, Orly Cobey. Orly and Thurmon had far more authority in Jasper Park than they could handle. They hunted together, played poker together, drank together, and because neither one could make a decision about anything, they consulted together, a perpetual committee of two. I think they must have seen the whole world through each other's eyes, having so little to see with on their own.

"Oh, sure, Noel be just just smilin ear to ear. He's got nothin better to do," my father continued in a high voice, bold and craven both. Maybe only once a year did my father get this mad now that he was sober. "Why bring Noel in on this? Why not tell him. . . . You tell him yourself, Thurmon. This is your baby. I'm not paid to go around –"

My mother stood by the sink, finger to her lips even though I was quiet, listening to the buzz and crackle of radio static and the thunderous lisping retorts of Thurmon Butters, who was up earlier than he liked to be and obviously still without his teeth.

You can live in a cabin miles from anywhere but you can never really get away from the likes of Thurmon Butters. Maybe that's what Mother was thinking when Father finally agreed to Thurmon's orders. He and Noel were off in the truck without any breakfast. I asked Mother where they were going and she told me to mind my own business. Go play with Delphine.

Dad and Noel had their rifles.

Nokom responded to this event with a grim smile, or what might have passed for a smile among white people. "Kuh!" she grunted. "Injun gonna soot a bear. Thinks he's gonna be a man, ah? Join up wit de posse."

"Noel and my Dad?"

Delphine said nothing. For a moment all I could hear was the blowing of the kettle.

"*Mikoskātēyihtamōwin*," Nokom muttered, not really to me or anyone in the dark kitchen. "*Mikoskātēyihtamōwin*." Trouble.

No one spoke, the kettle whispered, the dogs lay on the floor, heads on their paws, eyes rolling up red and mournful to watch us: Nokom whispering like the kettle, Delphine picking up her food, I shrugging at no one.

"*Maskwa*," muttered Nokom. "You better run."

For the longest time, I thought she meant Noel, until I learned that *Maskwa* in Cree meant bear.

There had been a mauling down at the CN station. Not a bad one either. A boy had gone and leaned on the snow fence at feeding time while he was snapping a picture. He fell head first into the bear welcoming committee, camera flying. The camera struck a cub on the nose, the cub set up a yowl, the nearest sow gave the boy a swat, and he screamed. I guess that boy must have put the panic into all those bears: a kicking screaming human-thing in their midst, one that hurts cubs when he's supposed to be feeding them. The sow took him by the shoulder, gave him a good shaking, and let him go, then lit off for the woods with a dozen other bears. The boy took ten stitches.

I've seen some people in my time, but let me tell you, this boy's father was something else. According to my dad, who got the story second-hand, this man was a grand poobah with the civil service. He had some pretty strong opinions about bears. They travelled in "packs" and this "pack" probably had rabies, every one of them; and if not, then they were still dangerous, and why didn't somebody do something before someone got killed?

Thurmon asked the man, "Like what?"

"Like shooting that bear before I have the lot of you fired for endangering people's lives."

"Which one?" asked Cobey. He always had an eagerness about him when it came to hunting things.

Well, they sort of thought it was a sow, because around cubs the sows get the most skittish. But Cobey himself claimed it was a big boar. No doubt Cobey was dreaming of bear hides. And of course Thurmon had some plans of his own. With his job on the line and that man from Ottawa looking over his shoulder taking down names, Thurmon Butters, with the help of his perpetual committee, made an administrative decision. "We'll get up a posse," he said to the man from Ottawa. "We'll get a posse, and you come in at the end of the week when the Injun's done his work, and by garsh," he said with a toothpicky smile, "you can have your pick of the hides."

Noel should never have gone into town that day. This is what happened. Thurmon Butters was very nervous about shooting what in all probability would be quite a few bears, though at the same time, very eager to do it. He just didn't want any screw-ups. Wounded bears, that is. If, after the first barrage, one or two of these wounded bears remained, he wanted to be sure there was someone present who was a good enough shot to finish them off before they made it into the trees; or who, if one or two bears actually made it into the trees, would have the nerve and the know-how to track them down and shoot them. Sergeant Cobey wasn't the least bit nervous. Likely he saw the whole thing as a glorious counterattack against the dark forces of nature. The more fire power the better. And they both needed someone to skin out the animals because when would there be another opportunity to get their hands on so many bear hides?

Noel Muskwa was the answer to both their prayers. But he had to be lured in. After all, he had little love for the town that was forever attempting to take his kids away, and he had no quarrel against bears. So my father was the key. Under threat of dismissal, he agreed finally to ask Noel to come along as a personal favour.

But why did Noel agree to participate in this supreme folly? He never did Father favours unless he felt like doing them, and he could not have felt much like doing this job: slaughtering a bunch of innocent animals and skinning them out. Seeing inside the hide of each animal the body of a man. Who knows? The body of an ancestor? Up north lots of Cree elders still refuse to kill bears.

I think Noel wanted recognition. Here was his chance to show these people who were in constant pursuit of his children that what he and his family did in the bush was important: the hunting, the skinning, the horsemanship, the bush lore that he taught his kids. His services for the town's respect. And when he arrived in Jasper with the tools of his trade, skinning knife and rifle, they'd see him as he really was. And they'd see he came in Joe Hetherington's half-ton. While my father was in his sober period, a lot of people respected him for the same reasons they had doubts about Butters and Cobey. So doing Father this favour might serve to kill two bears with one stone.

My God, what an awful way of putting that. But maybe in ways I can only begin to understand, that's just how it went.

Dad and Noel only just managed to make it into town before the road went all greasy from rain. There on the station platform were sixteen men with rifles. Several were Mounties and wardens but most were made into what Thurmon Butters called special deputies, and more than one or two pretty unhappy about getting roped into this caper. Roadblocks were set up to keep people away. Several horses stood patiently in the rain, one for Noel and the rest for the men who were to ride with Noel after the "stragglers," as Butters called them.

An hour or so before the Edmonton train was due in, several out-of-town photographers showed up. Thurmon Butters and Orly Cobey had discouraged this, but some people reckoned that if Ottawa was to know of their determination to keep the park safe for tourists, they may as well read it in the newspapers. The reporters raced out beyond the platform to where Noel was stationed, rifle in hand, on a borrowed horse, looking very dubious; looking, I imagine, as though by some mistake he had found himself fighting for the wrong side.

One of the photographers asked Noel if he didn't mind posing for some pictures in someone's borrowed buckskin jacket. The bears weren't due in for at least another half-hour. Noel told them if they didn't get out of the line of fire it would be their hides he'd be nailing to the barn that night. This put some people in a very shaky mood.

When the train pulled in that day, only seven bears showed up. Some people said it was the rain. I doubt that very much. My dad claimed it was the smell: desperation, fear, something like that. All those men with guns in the midst of a huge complicity bigger than the callousness of Orly Cobey, the perverse authority of Thurmon Butters, and the sheer sissiness of the man from Ottawa. You give a man a horse and gun and orders to kill, you line him up with a bunch of men with the same orders, I think you bring out something ugly that's been buried in all of them. I think the bears, even the ones imprudent enough to have shown up that day, could smell the smell of all that. They never reached their patch of grass and all that sweet Coca-Cola. They got past Noel Muskwa sitting quietly on his borrowed horse (perhaps he smelled just fine), they got past his mounted "deputies," and about halfway between Noel and the snow fence before they began to hesitate and sniff from side to side.

Noel was supposed to give the signal for the men on foot to fire, but he never got his chance. When Cobey saw the bears hesitate, he jumped the gun and yelled, "Now or never, boys!" and fired. About a dozen more rifles went off all at the same time. Noel's horse shied and he fell on the tracks with his boot in the stirrup. The men around him on horseback had to worry about their own horses. Some were thrown. There were bears in all directions, some of them injured, men firing wildly, bullets ricocheting, and for a minute they had too much in their sights to worry about Noel, whose horse was dragging him across the tracks, slamming him into cattle cars, whipping him around like a teddybear. Finally someone looked up and just shot his horse. I'm glad I wasn't there.

When Butters and Cobey called on their men to stop firing, there were four dead bears (three had escaped down Connaught Drive), one dead horse, and some injured men (two from being bucked off, one from a ricochet). Noel Muskwa was found half covered by his horse, cursing and coughing blood, his body utterly broken. Father stayed with him in the Jasper hospital for two days until Noel died. He wasn't really my father after that. He sort of fell apart.

I can't begin to imagine the impact of this tragedy on Nokom, Delphine, and all their kin. When you come right down to it, I only know how it hit me. The changes in Mother, Father, Delphine, and Nokom, for me, were like being told one day that the rules of the world had changed; nothing would be allowed to remain the same.

My father went back to his bottle and my mother took up with religion again. Father quit his job under Butters (who was fired soon after, along with Cobey) and returned to work in Jasper for the CNR (which he'd always hated and continued to hate). When my brother was born I had to "take care of Mother" by spending a lot of time around the house as a babysitter, for which I was bribed with Dinky Toys. Anyways, I'm getting ahead of myself.

Some people from town brought Noel home to Nokom's cabin. Dozens of his own people came in wagons to say goodbye to him. They threw up teepees and old grey canvas tents and stayed for several days. They laid him out in the cabin in a big wooden box on a couple of saw-horses. A priest sent Delphine and her cousins into the woods to hunt for Indian paintbrushes. They gathered armloads of them and laid them on the floor of the cabin.

I was too disturbed by Noel's death to be of much help, and so frightened that I even refused to go in and look. My mother said it was their way of saying goodbye to Uncle Noel, as she called him, and that I should go over there as our ambassador and pay my respects.

Later Delphine came over to fetch me. It was her job to keep the flies off her dad and lay the flowers on him, and she wanted me to help. I hid in the backhouse. Delphine

planted herself outside and said she wouldn't move until I
came out.

"I'm busy. Can't you see I'm busy?"

"Doin what?" she asked in a listless voice.

"None of your business."

"You've got to help, Barney. Nokom says."

"She's your grandmother, not mine."

"Your ma says so too. You got to help."

"I'm busy in here. Go way."

"You're just ascared. You don't have to be ascared."

"I am not scared."

"C'mon, Barney."

I refused to speak. My mother came out and said that if I
didn't unlock the door she'd go and get my father. No
answer. She got him and he said if I didn't come out he'd
tear the door off its hinges. I came out. Delphine took me
by the hand and we walked that immense hundred yards
from our backhouse to Nokom's place.

Noel was dressed in everyday clothes: fresh cowboy shirt,
jeans and boots, skinning knife and sheath on a wampum
belt of moose hide and a big silver buckle lying on his
chest. He looked smaller than life, shorter than his five foot
seven inches, much lighter than his hundred and seventy-
five pounds, the massive chest sunken. His cheeks sunken.
There were horrible gashes on his head but I don't remember where exactly. I remember how much, in spite of death,
he still looked like Uncle Noel, and that his face retained
that look of a man cursing. The same sparse black moustache, the same thrust-up lower jaw, the same deep lines
around eyes and brow that you see on the faces of so many
old hunters. But now the jaw, the lines, the moustache,
everything ordinary about his face, even the stained-log
pigment of his skin, conspired to look fierce.

I returned later and his body was covered with paintbrushes. Only that fervid face was showing, the red of the
flowers reflecting like new life on his cheeks. He was gath-

ering his strength to spring out of his box and do battle.

We kept the flies off his face and out of his ears, Delphine and I and one of her cousins, while all about us his people mourned in Cree and bits of French. Even the men wept and wailed openly.

Delphine developed a daydreaming look about her and bit her nails day after day until her fingers bled. On the last day of mourning, when Noel was getting pretty high, I found piles of faded paintbrushes on the floor of Nokom's cabin. Someone had come in and stolen Noel's beautiful belt, but left his skinning knife behind.

I don't remember much else. They took him away in a wagon and buried him somewhere north of Grand Cache. I don't think I saw much of Delphine that July. I spent my time reading war comic books. I have a sharp memory of one of them. A sergeant, who'd lost his entire platoon, stormed a big nest of Korean or Chinese soldiers and mowed them all down with a machine-gun. He was unshaven and had extremely white teeth. He yelled things like, "Take that, ya lousy gooks!" and the lousy gooks all went, "Aieee!" and died.

Someone from town gave Nokom a bear rug as an expression of the town's appreciation or bereavement or something.

A week or so later Mother found Nokom alone in her cabin, obviously distraught. Delphine was gone. "Where is she?" asked my mother.

"Nowhere," said Nokom.

"Who took her?" Mom asked.

"No one," she said. "He had a car."

2

I don't recall hearing of a bear getting shot anywhere in the park before that rainy day, except in the old days before

I was born, when no one rode through that country without a rifle and hunters came from the ends of the earth just to kill something big.

A few days after his bear ordeal was over I found Father staring at an old photograph, one that now hangs framed in my house. This photo says a lot to me about those early times in the park. It was taken by an unknown photographer near Jasper, a picture of four men leaning against a sidecar, circa 1910. Three of the men have big floppy Stetsons with the rims folded up at various rakish angles. These three also have bushy moustaches, the kind that collect food from every meal. They're all cradling rifles in their arms. The rifles are important somehow.

The fourth man holds a big revolver. He is unshaven, his whiskers light-brown or blond. He has a small moustache, wears a monocle, dirty tweeds, and a deerstalker. He's the only one smiling. He looks unhinged, nervous. If I were to guess, I'd say he was the boss out there, a remittance man who'd been cut off and fallen into a bottle, and retained some sort of deranged authority by flashing that six-shooter of his. This guess at least fits with the skimpy bits of information I have on him.

Behind the four men is a straggle of shacks and tents. The encampment looks scarcely more permanent than a bivouac, like they would stay there for some time, but like they were none too fond of their place.

At the edge of the photograph sits a fifth man, young, unarmed, an Indian. He has a child in his lap. It seems this man was not intended to be in the photo. He's only half interested in this show of arms. Perhaps he's disgusted with it, hiding his disgust. This is not apparent in the picture; this is me moralizing. But perhaps it's also the truth.

The man with the child on his lap is dressed in a shirt, trousers, and boots that conform to those of his fellow workers. The only difference is that he is wearing no hat while they are all wearing hats. I can't imagine these four men without their floppy hats or the deerstalker, their whiskers, or their various guns. And I can't imagine the man with the child on his lap growing whiskers, wearing a hat, or flashing a gun. My father claimed these men were a railway work crew on a siding west of Jasper.

The clothes on the man with the child on his lap bother me. They don't sit right on his body. I'm tempted to offer the usual theory: he's an Indian imprisoned in the white-man's ways. I know, I'm moralizing again. But I do have some inside information. The man holding the child is Etienne Muskwa, born during one of the last skirmishes of the Saskatchewan rebellion. They say he was descended from Big Bear's people. Etienne was a fine hunter, famous for it, and yet here he is unarmed with a kid on his lap. The child is Noel Muskwa.

When I look away from the photo, I retain an impression that the four men, especially the boss with the revolver, are scared, or at least very nervous. Perhaps they're bushed or something, the woods leaning in on them, sasquatches chasing them in their dreams. I think the crazy Englishman blew off Etienne Muskwa's hand with that gun of his. (I think so. Father told me that shortly after the bear episode when he'd taken out the photo. He was in his cups and very gloomy.) The crazy Englishman was my grandfather.

One night in bed, a week or two before we moved away from the lake forever, I found someone's hand in bed with me. It touched my face, plucked my ears, pulled my nose, brushed my eyelids, all this as light as a moth. I clenched and unclenched my right fist and I could feel it, so it wasn't my right hand. I drew my left hand out from beneath my leg, waved it around and felt it. I lay there with my hands in the air, opening and closing them as though milking an invisible cow. Neither hand was asleep. So what in God's name was this third one? A mouse? A dream? Etienne Muskwa's severed hand?

I opened my eyes and slowly sat up. I could make out the wooden Coke cases Father had nailed together for my dresser, my fishing rod leaning against the window, my baseball glove hanging on the wall.

Someone snickered.

It was him, I knew it, he'd come back for his hand. He was hissing, he smelled like a bear. "Sssss!" he went. And giggled.

Delphine. She stood behind my bed. (She always did have trouble with the "sh" sound.) I was wild with joy. She pounced on me and we rolled around the bed shushing each other and giggling in whispers.

"How long you bin standing there?"

"Bout a mont' or two."

"How'd you get in?"

"By there," she gasped, pointing to my open window. "I ran away. I'm not never goin back."

"What if they find you?"

"Nokom's got me hid in the daytime. Don't tell your mom and dad."

I stared and stared at her. She smelled rank. They'd cut her hair short, but otherwise she was the same old Delphine, the frog-faced grin, the eyes disappearing, the way she pulled her head in like a turtle when she laughed. We lay on the bed and whispered for a long time. She had walked the thirty-five miles from Jasper to Celestine the previous day. She claimed some of the sisters of the convent were trying to "get" her, whatever that meant. So each day Delphine slept on a shelf rolled up inside the bear hide the townspeople had given to Nokom. A man from social services and a church woman came to find her the next day. Nokom let them look around, pretending to speak only Cree. They went away empty handed.

Each day Delphine slept inside the bear hide and breathed in the musky smell of fresh bear. After a while this smell must have become normal to her. In fact, each night, when she snuck into my bedroom, she smelled overwhelmingly of bear. I'd have had nightmares, perhaps in dreams become that *Maskwa* so dreaded by campers.

Each night Delphine was awake and frisky. When Nokom nodded off to sleep she stole over to our cabin, crawled in my window, and woke me up. We were so quiet. It amazes me how quiet we must have been. We devised an animal game where words were unnecessary. We were a mama and papa bear. We arranged my blankets under the bed. This was our den. Inside the den we were safe. Outside it, however, collecting fish and coconuts and things, we had to be careful. Zulu warriors were everywhere. They'd spear you and eat you and make you stand all day memorizing things till you got them right. They had a witch doctor who spoke a funny language.

There were dangerous snakes beyond the den. Socks were poisonous snakes and Delphine's bluejeans were a python. Baseballs and rubber balls were coconuts and other fruit; shoes were fish. We always fed each other; we never fed ourselves. Zulus could come in through the bedroom door but they couldn't come in through the window. I kept wanting to shoot the snakes with my cap gun (unloaded, of course). I remember that. But Delphine would not allow this. We had to swat them with our paws. Delphine must have known that even the click of the hammer could have awakened my parents.

The Zulus had wiped out our tribe of bears, all except for some cubs. There were a few out there in the jungle and we had to find them and bring them home. My Bambi was one, my pillow another.

We'd always fall asleep in the den, and if I woke up first I'd rouse Delphine, help her to throw her clothes on, and pack her out the window before Nokom discovered our secret arrangement. Usually, though, I'd be the one to fall asleep first and wake up last beneath my bed, and in the morning Delphine would be gone and back inside her skin. Around that time I decided that when I was a little older I'd ask her to marry me. We'd go and live in Africa or somewhere, refuse to wear clothes or speak words, and never come back. I wonder if I ever told her that. I don't think so. It bothers me that I may never have told her that. Sometimes you wish things could have been different.

One day when Mother and Father were packing boxes for our big move and I was picking berries with Nokom, that man and woman came back. They searched Nokom's shelves. Maybe they spotted Delphine's foot sticking out of the bearskin or something like that. At any rate, they hauled her off in her sleep. Probably she didn't even wake up till she got down to Jasper. I came back with Nokom and Delphine was gone.

I had never felt so alone in all my life. I moped around for days and weeks. I would refuse to sleep in my bed, only under it, and when my mother insisted that I sleep in it, I would do so only if I could sleep with Nokom's bear hide. I spent hours in silent communion with Nokom. I began to follow her around each day, imitating her, asking her questions. She wasn't very responsive. One night I overheard Mother talking to Father near the corral when I was supposed to be asleep: "He's spending too much time over there. He's beginning to smell like them."

That September it was hot and dry, the fire hazard up, so they got Father to stay on at Celestine for a little longer. Some nights I heard Nokom moaning and muttering things in Cree. This went on through the late summer and early autumn. Sometimes I awoke to her monologues at four or five in the morning when it was still dark, which meant she'd been talking to thin air all night long. Her voice would drift across the clearing in a high croaking lament.

Dad got very tense. He had spotted a grizzly bear near the corral at twilight. Nokom's dogs chased it off, it was a big one. So he would sit around drinking whisky and listening. I was not allowed out after dark. Dad's rifle would lean against the door, and as he sat there, he would roll a 30/30 shell around and around in his hand, staring and listening. He reminded me of my grandfather's picture, the one he had shown me a few days after Noel had died. In spite of the dark and Father's bear vigil, Mother would occasionally put down her Bible and go over to visit Nokom, but Nokom would just go silent. When Mother left, Nokom would start up her monologue again and go all night long.

One night I heard her muttering outside my window. *"Tanewa, tanewa . . . napao?"* Then, *"Tanewa, tanewa . . . iskwasis?"* These were the words, or some of them. Where is he, the man? Where is the girl? Then softly, *"Tanu? Tanu?"* She said other things but I couldn't make them out, or if I could, I've forgotten them.

I looked out the window and saw her small figure heading slowly past the corral. A horse whickered. She went up past the horses into the trees. Another horse whickered, and another. From inside Nokom's cabin the dogs began to bark. In a minute or two there was an awful uproar. Father ran out in his longjohns. He had his rifle and was mad as hell. He hopped over to Nokom's cabin, opened the door, and all the dogs ran out. They raced into the trees the way Nokom had gone and raised a terrible racket.

None of us could figure out why Nokom had chosen to lock the dogs inside. In the daytime, they could come in and out as they pleased, but at night they had always slept outside.

The next night I woke up once more to Nokom's voice: *"Tanewa, tanewa?"* She went up back of our cabin and I threw on my clothes. I had this idea that maybe Delphine had come back. I'm sure I'd been praying for such a thing.

Nokom stood in the clearing, facing uphill toward the ridge, swinging this thing in her hand. All I could see on the ridge were some very big tree stumps, burnt-out Douglas firs, and a big boulder. In the dark, though, the tree stumps looked alive and massive, with stubby arms and legs. They looked like totem poles. I started to think about maybe going home. Under my bed or on it, there were always certain guarantees of safety.

Nokom's voice changed, it wailed high and cracked, a child-voice singing and weeping at the same time. I remember some of the words too, partly because I'd learned them from Delphine and her people, partly because they reminded me of other words. "*Sōskwāts*," she said, which means "for no reason"; "*Wanitipiskipayiw*," which means "it becomes dark." Noel's name was mentioned, and her daughter Annette's name, and "*awāsis*," meaning "the child."

It's funny, I don't remember many of the words but I still have dreams about her up there, wailing and swinging that thing at the tree stumps. In my dream she's on the ridge with her back to me, but at an angle. I'm in the trees. The top of the ridge is about thirty feet away. There's the big burnt-out tree stump, then a boulder, then another tree stump and that's all. And Nokom waving this thing like a plumb bob at those objects. There must have been some moonlight too, because otherwise I wouldn't have seen the boulder move, which is exactly what it did. A big head sort of grew out of that boulder, and as Christ is my witness, it just stood up as huge as those two tree stumps. Right then Nokom gave a final cry and heaved her thing at that boulder with all her might. The boulder caught it, ate it, and I fainted dead away on the spot.

Some of this can be explained. I've done some thinking about that night. Nokom likely went up that hill with what must have been a chunk of meat in her hand, a chicken maybe, or a dead rabbit. There's no boulder on that ridge between the two burnt-out stumps, so it doesn't take a genius to figure out that my boulder was a very large grizzly. I mean, old Nokom *knew what she was looking for*. That's why she kept shutting the dogs up in the cabin. She was out hunting up that big old bear. She found him and fed him. When he ate the rabbit or whatever, there wasn't ten yards between them.

Why she sought out this bear is another question. Bears are sacred to those people. You take it from there. I'm not one to speculate about religion, much less someone else's religion. My mother spent the last half of her life in the arms of Jesus and only got out of bed to go to church. My little brother Darryl was born in the midst of her voyage back to Jesus and he still hasn't recovered from it. All I have to do is swear a few times or criticize our parents for their ostrich-like tendencies and Darryl gives me this look of his, as if to say, I feel sorry for you, Barney. I really do. So endeth the lesson.

I've kept a souvenir from that night, my jean jacket, made by G.W.G. The cloth is very tough, wears like iron, as they say. Right now it's hanging on my hiking stick just next to my typewriter. I was wearing that jacket when I got dragged down the hill. It was like a dream. Either I couldn't move out of fear, or I was still half in a faint. But I got dragged down that hill, face downwards, by the collar of my jean jacket. Dragged down the hill and dropped on the steps of Nokom's cabin. You take it from there. I don't want to give the impression that some childloving bear fresh from an engagement with Walt Disney Studios just picked me up and took me home. That's approximately what I used to think when I was a boy. (What can I say? I read Tarzan comics like scripture.) In fact, if some altruistic bear did bring me down and drop me on the steps, why didn't the horses in the corral and the dogs in the cabin make a sound? But they didn't. If they had, my father would have been over there in a second.

But if it were Nokom who dragged me down the hill (assuming for a moment that a one-hundred-pound granny could do such a thing), why would she have dragged me past our cabin and dropped me on the steps of her own? You can't get down to Nokom's cabin from the slope without passing ours.

I remember several things about my trip down the slope: the snuffling sound of laboured breathing right in my ear, a sour musky smell of warm breath on the back of my head and neck, the feeling of being half-strangled by the collar of my jean jacket, and the sensation of being born along by something very strong, extremely strong, through the brush and up the steps.

I wonder, of course, how much of this is my own invention. I pick up my jacket and hold it to the light. In the collar are two holes about five inches apart. I stick my thumb and finger through these holes and wiggle them.

You see my problem here: I don't know what to make of this event. To write it down like this, as I remember it, makes me feel as though I've crossed some kind of line.

Nokom's people took her up north of Cache Creek and we never saw her again. Apparently she died not long after leaving Celestine Lake. We moved and Darryl was born. The rest of this story can be read in summary in the *Jasper Herald*. The back issues are in the Jasper archives. This one is September 30, 1953, one year after my bizarre trip down the mountainside.

GIRL CARRIED OFF BY GRIZZLY

RCMP and armed parks employees are combing the bush today around Willow Creek in search of Delphine Muskwa, ten years old, of St. Theresa Residential School. According to a playmate, Barney Hetherington, also ten years old, young Delphine was grabbed by a marauding grizzly.

The two were playing in the Hetheringtons' backyard when the attack occurred. Little hope is held out that the girl will be found alive.

The bear was seen entering town by several children in a nearby playground. They ran immediately to the nearest building, the Athabasca Hotel, and reported their sighting to patrons there. Some men investigated but failed to spot the bear.

It was seen leaving town by a group of girls who were returning from a hike near Patricia Lake. One girl, Amy Cobey, told reporters that the bear dragged the screaming

victim across the Patricia Lake Road and into the bushes by
the Willow Creek culvert.

Parents are advised to keep a close watch on their children.
According to the former Superintendent, Mr. Thurmon Butters, "a killer bear may strike again." He claims what the park
needs is "a new policy on bears."

The victim is the daughter of Noel and Annette Muskwa,
both deceased, native Indians who resided for many years
near this town.

You can talk to reporters till you're blue in the face, but
they rarely get it down right. I object to words like "marauding," "screaming victim," and "dragged." That's not
how it happened. I know, I was there.

To understand what happened when the bear came you
need to know what lead up to it. With Delphine, I mean.
With Nokom gone, Mother and Father had applied to become her foster parents. The minister of Mother's church
thought it would be a good idea, part of a program to get
Father off the bottle and Mother out of bed: a daughter for
my mother, who had once expressed a preference for
daughters. The Sisters of St. Theresa didn't seem to mind
either, even though Mother and Father weren't Roman
Catholics. A series of visits were set up.

One day, it must have been on the weekend, two sisters
showed up and told Mother that Delphine was out in the
car. "Give her time to come around," one of them cautioned. I was delegated to play with Delphine. Apparently
the sisters and my mother had gotten together on this. I
was to play with Delphine all day and never once let her
out of my sight. Very solemnly I agreed to this arrangement and Delphine was led in by both the sisters.

She was wearing new jeans, a new shirt, and runners, but
what caught my eye was a huge belt tied to her waist, one
too thick for the loops on her jeans. It had a big silver
buckle. It was Noel's belt. There she stood between the two
nuns, hanging from their hands, looking distracted and
perhaps, too, a bit sulky, gazing back over her shoulder

into the distance. This is how a prisoner might have looked who was coming to trial in a police van. The nuns looked nothing like cops, though. I mean they were just doing their job and with Delphine it couldn't have been easy. Stand up, Delphine. Say hello to Mrs. Hetherington. Don't slouch. That sort of thing. She rolled her eyes upward at her bangs and stood, choosing not to focus on us or anyone else. She made a silly frog-face at no one in particular.

"You want to see my trucks?" I said.

"Wanna see my twucks?" she said in a baby voice to the ceiling.

I led her out to the sandbox. Her hand was limp with indifference. We knelt in the sand and I gave her a car. She put it on her head, bowed, and it fell to the sand.

"*Kreegah!*" I cried. "*Bundolo!*"

She picked up my car and threw it backwards over her head. It landed next to the snow fence Father had recently erected.

In that same wilful baby voice she said, "I'm too little to play with you."

They brought her a week or two later and she seemed to have changed. She wore a dress and a pink barrette in her hair, but once more Noel's belt around her waist. This time she looked us all in the eye, stood up straight, refused the sisters' hands. When we greeted her at the door she bobbed with Teutonic stiffness and walked right in.

"How come you got all this stuff?" she asked when she and I were alone.

"What stuff?"

"All this stuff," she said, waving a hand nowhere in particular. I think we were in the front room. Our home was a very modest war vintage pre-fab, sparsely furnished, owned by my grandmother Sharples. I think Delphine was referring to the things in our front room, pictures painted by my grandmother, framed photographs of birds, Indians, and mountains; the brass lamp next to Father's easy-chair; an old couch Grandmother Sharples had re-covered; an old radio in a wooden casing; a box of my Dinky Toys; things that seemed to come with moving to town. "You should give it all to Jesus," she said.

"What for?"

"Because He's comin back."

"Let's go outside," I said. I figured maybe we could play a little catch. Delphine was good at catch; she threw like a boy. She looked at the implements in our shed (Father's tools, his old horse gear, Mother's gardening stuff, etc.).

"You got so much stuff. You should give it away. You should give it to the Doukhobors."

"Let's play catch," I said.

She looked around the shed for a moment, then came out and stood in the centre of the sandbox. "Jesus ever talk to you?" she asked.

"Nope."

"He talked to me. Once when we was singin and once in my room."

I'd had it up to here with religion, even then. As far as I was concerned it was about as beneficial as Father's imbibing, just another source of embarrassment for me at school. Why couldn't they be like other people's parents? "That's all a load of horseshit," I said.

"What's that supposed to mean?" she said, spoiling for a fight. I guess I was too.

"I got better things to do than go into a church and pray to a guy hanging there with his guts spilling out." I meant crucifixes and pictures of saints with bleeding hearts. I'd seen them in the chapel where Delphine went. They were awful. They made me think of Noel oozing blood beneath his horse. At least at Mother's church there was no blood and guts, only pictures of Jesus in the prime of his life. He looked like someone out of *Prince Valiant* comics, except of course he had no armour. I think I mentioned that to Delphine.

"We got Holy Water," she said.

"What's that?"

"The Pope blesses it and then God blesses it. There's a bunch of it in our chapel. I could drink some if I wanted to."

"So why don't you then?" When you come right down to it, I was being as obnoxious as I could possibly be.

"Maybe I will. Maybe I'll be ready when He comes. It's plain as day that you won't, so never mind. He's comin and it could be real soon. Any day, so there."

It never occurred to me that she may have been trying to tell me something else: that if I did prepare myself, she and I would go to the same place, that we belonged together, like being back in Africa, or wherever she imagined Paradise to be. But she was talking to me as though I were *her* foundling, abandoned like someone's bastard on her doorstep.

The last time Delphine got brought over, I was in my room stalling. Father had to drag me out and haul me down to the sandbox, mad as hell at both of us. It was like having to view the body of Noel again, except this time I had to contend with a live Muskwa.

She was down on her knees in the sandbox. It was beginning to rain. She was praying. Off in the distance I could hear some kids yelling things. I remember thinking, Jesus, I don't want those kids to find me here with this Bible-thumping Indian kid. It sounded like they were coming my way. They'd probably be from my school and here was Delphine mumbling to God in the sandbox.

"There," she said, took off Noel's big belt, and stood up. She held the belt like a snake by the tail and began swinging it. "This is what the priest does with his therble," she said. She meant that censer they use, the thing that holds the incense. It reminded me of Nokom with her dead rabbit or whatever; it gave me the creeps. The kids were getting closer; I could hear them yelling.

"Delphine? Don't do that. Delphine?"

She kept swinging her belt, the big silver buckle downward, and humming a weird Indian song. I got scared and yelled at her, and the kids I kept hearing got closer and closer. *"It's going down the lane!"* they shouted.

"Stop it!" I cried. "Stop it! Stop it! Stop it!"

She stopped, and fastened the belt around her waist. There was a noise.

We both looked up at the snow fence and the garbage cans beyond: a huge frosted hump loomed up, then a pale yellow head, flat like a big spade, pig snout and unseeing eyes that seemed to burn. It didn't actually hit the snow fence, it just sort of moved and the entire fence came down like cardboard in a gust of wind. It came up with a woofing sound, like the biggest Sumo wrestler in the world, sniffing.

I remember screaming but not *us* screaming. Just screaming, as if everything in our yard, the ruined fence and the house included, were screaming out at this colossus that walked through things we thought belonged there; and Delphine and I performed in slow motion our last act together: I in the sandbox reaching out to her, she by the shed falling towards me with her arms out – reaching for me? I don't honestly know. It came down over her gently, and with the delicacy of a great regent nibbling on a grape, closed its mouth on the belt and hauled Delphine into the air. Her expression was that of a kid tobogganing down a mountain slope with an avalanche behind her. The bear swung back toward the ruined fence and lumbered down the lane.

"A grizzly!" cried one of the kids nearby. "It's a grizzly bear!"

Note: it never dragged her, it carried her. And she never screamed. And they only found her clothes. You can ask those Mounties and wardens. Ask them if they found one piece of flesh or even a drop of blood.

The last time I really tied one on was a pretty sobering experience. Darryl and his wife were over. He is blond, fat, successful and unctuous, a mama's boy who made me feel in those days too much like Papa's boy. He kept staring at the photograph of the four bewhiskered railroaders and their guns.

"Here's to our dear grandfather," I said, and wanting to shake out some of the complacency from Darryl's face, I added, "He blew Etienne Muskwa's hand off with that six-gun of his."

"I know," said Darryl. "Mom told me."

"Blew the man's hand to kingdom come. Thought he was a bear," I added morosely.

"Like father, like son," Darryl said.

"What's that supposed to mean?" I must have sounded surly. The wives started looking pretty nervous.

Darryl didn't even blink. He said, "Come on, Barney. You mean to tell me you never knew?"

"Knew what?" I said.

"It was our father who shot that other Indian's horse from under him. That's what did him in, what's his name, Noel. Didn't he ever –"

"How do you know?"

"Mom told me."

"Jesus Christ," I said.

"Amen," he said.

I knew he was telling the truth. It would've been just like our mother to tell Darryl and not tell me. Maybe in some way I'd known this fact all along. But Darryl's little revelation went through me like a bolt from the other side of the universe. Another look at the photograph confirmed it for me. It. Something connecting all three generations of us. A look we Hetheringtons get when we've learned something we didn't want to know.

Something about the bush. One night a group of men are sleeping around a campfire. A paw reaches out from the wilderness, crossing the line between the Vast Other and you, fumbles for your shoulder, you grab the revolver and fire again and again. Men leap from their bedrolls, a

whole tribe of bears roars out in brute pain: *Mamuskach!*
Uy! Uy! Uyiwakekin! and there it lies by the campfire,
spurting blood. Clenching like a dying spider. Maybe he
only wanted to cover your shoulder with your blanket, but
you shot his hand off. You repeat this act again and again
in a film that winds through your head until you die. Or
maybe your film is the one where you shoot your friend's
horse and it falls on him. Or maybe, in the most recent
version, you repudiate the only friend you had, send her
back into her own solitude with such finality that (after
your brother has gone, leaving you alone with your very
last drink), when you play it back, the whole wilderness
rears up to rebuke you.

Life on
the Edge

A long time ago my wife and I and the Henskes went to
Banff over Christmas for some skiing. On New Year's Eve
something happened that I've never forgotten.

We had reservations for supper at the nearest restaurant
to our motel. My friend Wally and my wife Daphne had
gone to their respective washrooms and I was there with
Wally's wife Arlene waiting to order. Our waitress was a
pretty brunette from Quebec City. I was pretending to be
interested in what Arlene was saying, but I was depressed
and I didn't know why.

Something was missing. It was New Year's. Check. We
were all four of us young, not yet thirty, healthy, and more
or less happy. Check. Daphne had a good job, so she
hadn't become housebound and schitzy like Arlene tended
to get. Daphne was still cute and freckled, though not a
knockout like Arlene. But, still. And like Wally, I had what
most people would call a future. In fact, I'd just been
promoted.

So. What was missing?

Arlene was droning away, something about the hassle of buying a bedroom suite. She has this very deep sexy voice, a hostess voice. But if you encouraged her, she tended to talk non-stop. Actually, sometimes she'd get on my nerves. "I mean, *I've* got *my* stuff left over from *my* apartment, and Wally still has *his* stuff from *his* old apartment, and it's *perfectly* good furniture, so . . ."

A waitress swung by and I just caught a glimpse of her. Something about the heavy way she strode into the kitchen, something sumptuous about the haunches. And I thought, she reminds me of someone. She really reminds me of someone.

And then, like I say, I was depressed and I didn't know why, and Arlene was going non-stop about her bedroom furniture and I was pretending to be very sympathetic. In my line of work you learn to do that. Part of the problem, I began to realize, was that in the old days on campus, Arlene didn't talk about things like that. She used to be a lot of laughs. Unless I'm mistaken, she used to flirt with me.

Then it hit me, a sort of print-out of our destinies: here was this lovely-looking woman talking to me by candlelight. We would never again banter about who was hustling whom in the study hall or why so-and-so got so bombed at the Pan-Hell exchange. After supper the four of us would go to a party filled with people like us, more or less happily married. We would drink good booze, though likely not a lot of it. We would have a gang kiss at midnight in some sort of parody of promiscuity. The embraces between Arlene and me would not be lingering like they were in the good old days. Arlene had developed a sort of post-marital hug that allowed her to preserve a space between my body and hers. Daph and I would go back to our motel room and to bed, perhaps have sex, or more likely not have sex, and it would be 1972. And it would be the same in 1973. And that was all.

"I mean, what would *you* do?"

"I'd sell it. Sell the whole shooting match."

Arlene looked at me as though I'd said, Donate it all to the Workers' Solidarity Fund or something like that. "Well, of *course*, but how? I mean, the auctioneers will rob you *blind*. . . ." And yappity yappity, off we go again.

I raised my beer glass and squinted around the rim to see if the larger waitress would come out again. She didn't come out, she didn't come, but the name of the girl she reminded me of *did* come out. "Gladys Hornby!" I said, and Arlene said, "What?"

Save your nickels, save your dimes,
Better get ready for tougher times
'Cause Gladys isn't gratis any more.
Well, there was a time when love was free
But now it's comin' C.O.D.
'Cause Gladys isn't gratis any more.

Gladys sings this to the tune of "Five Foot Two," grinds it out by the bonfire in a voice that looks forward to Mama Cass. She holds my ukelele up to her breasts like a newborn infant, strums and sways, head thrown back, and all that wild hair . . .

A summer night, circa 1960, somewhere north of Banff and west of Lake Louise, a campground on the Great Divide. If you're from B.C., you stumble off into the bush in an easterly direction to piss on Alberta. If you're from Alberta, you go in the opposite direction and piss on B.C. If you're from Saskatchewan, you try to piss on both of them, and if you're from east of there, you don't give a damn.

I am nineteen. My parents christened me Hubert, refer to me as P.K. (the Personality Kid). But they are not here, where everyone calls me Hugh. I am a bellboy at Deer Lodge and surrounded by people who know what good times are all about. Gladys is with an older guy from Australia. After a while, after the rowdy phase of the singsong, she will disappear with him. Somewhere beneath a blanket they will roll in the agony of creation, as Gladys puts it. If she were back in the city, Gladys Hornby would be more discreet. Well, a little more discreet.

The singsongs have become ritualized. I always bring my ukelele for Gladys. Wally always brings his guitar. Someone always plops an open case of beer at their feet. Sleeping bags and blankets go down all around us and we bunch in by the fire. We never start with bawdy songs; they're for later when everyone's oiled up a bit. We start with songs about black people who get drunk and get into a fight and someone has to go their bail, or who sweat all day in the cottonfields. In a transport of pious brotherhood we become one with these commonfolk down south. It has something to do with Civil Rights and how the other half lives, out there on the edge and all that, and we demonstrate just enough moral outrage to make our parents wonder if the days of capitalism aren't numbered.

Gladys Hornby never seems to *get* any of this folk stuff. She'd just as soon begin with "Roll Me Over in the Clover" and proceed to the one about the four and twenty virgins who go down to Inverness.

I am somewhere off in the bushes peeing where I think British Columbia might be, listening to the singing and looking up at the stars, knowing that if there's an Action Central anywhere in the universe, we are it. And I get one of those thoughts that, if you're tight enough, feels so profound you just stand there with your mouth and your fly open while it courses through you like a train: *I can be anyone I want to be* . . . and whistles down the tracks into a tunnel through the mountains. I turn and stumble over a pair of blanketed bodies.

"Next time point it the other way!" Gladys's voice. The way the words foam out of her mouth.

"Gladys, do you realize we can be anyone at all?"

Her man from down under mumbles something beneath the blanket about dying.

"No, no, seriously. It just came to me. We can be anyone. We can be Elvis."

"Peace orf, Hugh," says her friend. "Give us a brike."

"No, seriously, I mean it. It came like a flash."

Gladys detaches herself from her friend's embrace, hauls on her sweater. What did she say? She takes my face in both her hands, gives me a slobbery kiss, and says, *You only say that, Hugh, you only say that . . . because . . .*

Because why? I've blocked it out.

"Of course, we could just *store* it all, but do you have any idea how much it *costs* to store a small amount of furniture?"

I was rescued from responding to this weighty question by the return of Daphne. The four of us sat facing man to man and woman to woman in a nice flutter of candle-light. Wally squinted at his menu. "Excuse me, Miss," he said to the waitress. "What's in this shish kebab?"

"If I tell you, do you promise not to barf?"

We all gaped at the waitress towering above us in the dark. It wasn't the French girl this time. Her face flickered and she flashed a huge grin, a mouth bulging with teeth. Daphne shrieked, "Gladys Hornby!"

Arlene gasped, "My *God*, Hugh just mentioned your *name*."

"See?" I said. "I've just conjured her."

"That does it," said Wally. "I'm gonna go for the shish kebab."

Gladys gave him a very intimate look. "That'll cost ya, Wally."

Gladys Hornby always went too far. It was common knowledge that on a first date the most any guy could expect was a dry sampling of curt Protestant kisses. But no sooner were Gladys and her date settled into someone's back seat than she was panting away like an asthmatic hound. She changed the tone of things. Not because she was wilful. She wasn't wilful; she was just out of control.

Having a good time meant being on the way to having a better time.

According to Daphne, Gladys seemed to miss the whole point. The point was to comport yourself in such a way as to become irresistible to some guy with a future. "To get a good one," as she once put it. The sisters in Daphne's sorority learned to flutter, but not too much; they learned to prattle, the way Daddy loved to hear; to walk from the knees down in tight skirts and high heels as though it were the most natural way in the world to walk; to study the interiors of the best homes and find out what Real Quality was; to cook elaborate meals but avoid eating them. Sex was the reward for a boy who ate his main course. The main course was marriage.

Anyway, there was Gladys, big as life, and as in the summers of old, still a waitress. "You people!" she squawked. "You haven't changed a bit!" She placed my soup in front of me. "Baby Huey, you're still skinny as a rail." That was true. I've never been able to gain weight.

"Baby Huey!" cried Daphne. "I haven't heard that in ten years!"

Neither had I, not since I'd graduated. I tried my soup. It was lukewarm and much too salty. I would have sent it back, but I didn't want to make trouble for Gladys.

Baby Huey.

"And look at LaBonza stuffing his face as usual," Gladys went on. "I bet you still wear cowboy boots. Let's see." She flipped up the tablecloth and, sure enough, Wally was wearing his cowboy boots. "And here's Arlene, still the greatest body on the campus. And after how many kids?"

"Two," Arlene said, and smiled self-consciously.

When Gladys left, Daphne said, "My soup's cold."

"Oh, Baby Huey will take charge," Wally roared, much too loudly.

"Enough outa you, LaBonza," said Arlene, like the Arlene of old.

"How come I never had a nickname?" Daphne asked.

"Because you were always so cute!" said Arlene.

I started thinking about bodies. How Wally just got fatter and bigger, and how it never seemed to matter. He carried it all so well. And Arlene with her bouncy long body. She was an exercise and diet nut. Everywhere men ogled her. And Daph and me, the long and the short of it. She was about five foot two and still weighed about a hundred and five pounds. And me, I'm six one and I've never managed to get much past a hundred and fifty. And Gladys Hornby: a bit bigger around the hips, a bit rounder everywhere. At sorority dances her body always seemed stuffed into her formal gown.

She wasn't the fastest waitress I'd ever seen, but of course staying on schedule was never her strong suit. She was always the last one in for curfew at Residence. If it was one o'clock, she'd show up at five after and wonder why the front doors were locked. She always drank too much, swore too much, lost clothes, earrings, shoes, and showed up at the beach with hickeys and bruises in the funniest places.

I think, if she hadn't felt compelled by the laws of respectability to be friends with all of us, she might have been happy. But we held her back, admonished her, kept her in what we imagined to be her place. We also liked her quite a lot. In fact, we counted on her to be outrageous. It seemed to be up to all of us to remind Gladys that there were, after all, limits to behaviour, and her job to remind us that these limits ought to be pushed.

Why do I keep saying "us"? *I* was the one who told Gladys (with all the wisdom of my virginity) that free love was a symptom of a sick society. My tone on this occasion must have been so unctuous I have all but blotted out the incident. She accused me of being a crypto-Christian, a word I'd never heard. So I denied it.

Is it possible that I was such a self-righteous twit back then?

It is possible.

I used to moralize at Gladys in the student coffee lounge,

then launch into lewd speculations with the guys at the fraternity house over her latest hickey.

Her mouth. I can never forget her mouth. The teeth protrude rather prominently, the lips are plump and obey the outward bulge of her teeth. Straight beautiful teeth that cannot entirely be contained by her mouth. Wally used to say her mouth was made for kissing and sucking things. I should mention that she was a good student, won scholarships all through university, but I keep coming back to her body: her cheeks, arms, breasts, the whole thing so soft and bountiful, Nature seemed to be conspiring with the boys to get poor Gladys into trouble.

The salad was pathetic. Brown spots all over the lettuce, and almost nothing but lettuce. Daph had ordered a Caesar salad and she got the same crap as us. Well, we waited and waited. Once in a while there'd be this noise from the kitchen, someone yelling about something, and we were all just drooling with hunger. Wally was looking pretty mean. When he's hungry he's like a big infant. "If I don't get some goddam service around here," he said, and Arlene gave him this very nervous look.

Finally Gladys returned to our table. She smiled but you could see she was pretty upset about keeping us all waiting. "Things are pretty hairy in there," she said, more than once, and kept putting her hand over her mouth, the way little kids do when someone's done something bad.

Gladys's hands are very shapely. So are her feet. Hands and feet both are large, long, and fine, perfectly shaped. When she came to the pool at Lake Louise, I used to look at her hands and feet. I just remembered that. Let's face the facts here: I miss Gladys Hornby.

Finally she came back, she had our supper, it was almost midnight, Wally had this menacing look on his face, Arlene had the hiccups, Daphne was like a high-tension wire, and I was so far beyond hunger I was half asleep. Some New Year's. But there was our dinner. Wally's shish kebab was mostly burnt on one side and my salmon raw and red in the middle, but we managed to lace into it. There wasn't a whole lot of conversation. A belch now and then from Wally and a hiccup from Arlene. Someone at another table started to sing "Auld Lang Syne," and gave up after a while.

Gladys was there when we paid the bill. She apologized up and down but Wally stiffed her anyway. He had principles about certain things. He said to me he liked to pay for service, and, friend or no friend, fair was fair. We got down onto the street, Arlene had forgotten her purse. Wally pounded back up the stairs for it. A few minutes later he came down shaking his head and gave Arlene her purse.

"What was going on up there?" I asked, and Wally said, "Baby Huey, me boy, let's go and pour us a drink."

This is what he told us back at the motel: "I go right into the kitchen, see, and out comes their boss, he's been rakin them over the coals somethin fierce, and there's Gladys sittin on the goddam floor. She's bawlin her eyes out, she doesn't even see me. And here's this French number, she's givin shit to the cook. Longhaired guy. Turns out she's shacked up with him. And Gladys yells out, 'Every time I start to feel something for a guy, off he goes. It happens every goddam time.' "

"Oh, my *God*," says Arlene. "Do you mean that cook was having it on with *both* of them?"

"No-no. It's some other guy. The cook is drunk. That's why we had to wait so long for our dinner. Gladys had to cook it all herself and she doesn't know dick-all about cookin in a place like that. The boss is pissed off, the cook is just plain pissed, the French girl is reamin out the cook, and Gladys is bawlin out, 'I don't have anyone,' and all I'm after is Arlene's purse!"

"What did you do?" I asked.

Wally got a naughty look on his face. "I just yells out 'Happy New Year.' "

Daphne cracked up but Arlene looked scandalized.

"The French number, she's in no mood for fun and

games, she just throws Arlene's purse in my general direction."

"Did you check the contents?" Daphne asked.

"Nothing's missing," said Arlene.

The party we were going to rumbled in the room above us, a swanky affair. None of us seemed quite ready to join it.

"Well," said Daphne, "when you give it all away as many times as she did, I mean, let's face it, you take the consequences."

Arlene piped up. "She could have a man. She's still nice looking. She could take off a few pounds. It's not like she could have her choice, but she could have a man if she wanted one."

"Yes," said Daphne, "she just needs to take care of herself a bit more."

"Do you think she's all right?" I asked.

"She was always up and down. You remember," said Daphne.

"You can say that again," said Wally with a smirk. Arlene gave him a look.

After the Henskes had left, Daphne asked me, "Are you still worried about Gladys?" She'd changed into a blue dress and shoes. She looked real nice. All that red hair up in a roll.

"Yeah."

"This is going to sound catty of me but I'm going to say it anyway. She brought this on herself. She's always brought it on herself. If you sleep with hogs enough, you end up smelling like them."

"Where on earth did you pick up that one?"

"That's not the point," she said and looked up at me. Her glasses caught the light, like blank TV sets. She seemed to be someone else, a stranger.

"I keep thinking she needs someone to talk to."

"So, you want to go back to that . . . dive . . . and hold her hand?"

"I had considered it."

"It's snowing out. It's past one in the morning. They've probably all gone home."

"Wally said she was sitting on the kitchen floor."

"So?"

"Nothing."

"Hugh, Gladys Hornby has always done what Gladys Hornby wanted to do. If she was so hot on getting married she'd have gotten married, instead of going to bed with every Tom, Dick, and Harry."

"And Wally."

Daphne did a double take. "I rest my case," she said and click-click-clicked out of the room in her high heels. I couldn't get over the fact that she looked like someone else. Even her freckles looked different.

"I'll see you up there," I called out, but she didn't answer.

It was a short walk back. The night was mild. The snow fell almost vertically in big downy flakes. When I reached the door of the restaurant, an old guy was just leaving. He was very short and had a bad limp. He must have been some sort of caretaker. I wanted to sound casual. "Happy New Year," I called out.

"Ya-ya," he said, and locked the door behind him.

"I'm looking for Gladys," I told the man.

"She's gone home."

"Is she all right?" I asked, and he shrugged.

We stood around shifting our weight from one foot to another, then he gestured at an old black Dodge. "Chump in," he said. "I take you past there, ya?"

"Super," I said, and off we went into the snow.

I was perfectly aware that I was going to catch it from Daphne when I got back. She'd give me a real sang-froid special, go all silent and twitchy. We'd pass several days avoiding each other, she'd spend about a hundred hours on the bedroom phone with her know-it-all sister in Calgary, and maybe in a week we'd be back to normal.

The car glided through the storm, the snow fell heavily, the old man's windows were slow to defrost. I think we crossed a bridge. "Are we still in town?"

"Ya-ya."

I could hardly see a thing. Just the road ahead, a couple of white ruts. "Have we left town?"

"Ya-ya."

"Which is it?"

"Vitch?"

"Are we still in Banff or have we left?"

He pondered this like a philosophical problem. He was dwarfed by the steering wheel, gripped it like the horns of a Brahma bull, and tilted his chin away up to see out the windshield. "Ve're not in town, ve're not owt of town."

"Where are we, then?"

"Ve are on z'etch."

"Mr. . . . ah . . ."

"Schaumgummi," he said, the gummi part pronounced "goomy."

"Mr. Schaumgummi, where exactly are we going?"

"Liddle further."

"But the location, I mean, where exactly . . ."

"*La Bohème*," he said, and geared down around a hairpin turn, jerking a glance at me. "You a friend von Gladys?"

"Yep. More than ten years."

"Gladys hat a rough week, hm? She hat a really shiddy time of it. First her boyfriend dumps her, then he fires her. He owns that restaurant. First he dumps her, then he fires her. He fires all three of them."

"Why?"

"Because he's sonoffapitch and because the other waitress don't vant to go to bed with him. They are all of them Gladys's beeble, ya? Zo he fires them."

The car glided like a sleigh up the narrow road. Schaumgummi took the turns very slowly. The road levelled off and the snow continued to fall. How he could see through all of this I have no idea. Up here the wind swirled the flakes and exploded them all around us. But still the old black Dodge drifted over the roads. Finally we stopped at a very long driveway with big trees on either side and a broken metal gate. There were no car tracks leading in, I could see that much.

"You go in there," said Schaumgummi.

"But what if I can't get in?"

"Door's never locked. Go ahead." Then he pointed in the other direction. "Bempf is down there. If the road is too far for you, go down the path on your bum, hm?"

I got out onto the road. The storm swirled around me. "Mr. Schaumgummi, if I paid you twenty bucks, would you wait and drive me back?"

"Go," he said with finality, and his car purred off into the storm.

The driveway wound through the trees, and soon I was out of the wind, following some people's tracks. Gladys's beeble? Ahead of me were two pinpoints of light. I wondered what sort of beeble would live away up here, and whether Gladys hadn't gotten in with the wrong crowd.

Up ahead was a large house, an old three-storey job. It was made of slate and mortar, the kind you see on the Banff Springs Hotel. I followed the tracks in the snow right up to the big front verandah. The outside light shed some feeble rays on an old tin sign with red letters: *La Bohème*. I tried knocking a few times. The door finally opened from the impact of my pounding, so I went on in. The catch didn't work and much of the house, it seemed to me, was on its last legs. I couldn't see much, but what I could see looked pretty shabby. "Gladys!" I whispered. Not a sound. The house was chilly. It smelled of wood-smoke, ski wax, incense, many other things I couldn't identify. A white cat came forward from somewhere down the hallway, mewed, and leapt up an old creaky staircase that I hadn't noticed. I followed it. I couldn't see very well, but the second floor seemed unoccupied. I whispered Gladys's name but no one stirred. The cat stood on the landing by a window. It leapt up the stairs and tore down again, chasing an imaginary mouse, then raked the rug with its front claws. I knelt to pet it, but it raced up the stairs again to the third floor, so again I followed. The smell of incense grew stronger, and as I tiptoed around the last corner of the third-floor corridor, I saw the white rump of the cat disappear through a lighted doorway. Gladys had always liked cats, so I felt this had to be her room.

But I hesitated. This was no longer a mission of mercy. In fact, I was now at the mercy of this house's inhabitants with their threadbare sense of decor and their Bohemian ways. I couldn't, for instance, walk up to one of these people, slap him on the back and say, Hi, Hugh's the name, I'm in advertising. It was now more like an adventure. A blizzard on the outside and what appeared to be a house full of pariahs on the inside.

I crept up to the door and gently nudged it open. A candle was burning on the dresser. It gave off a nice orange glow. On a large mattress with the cat were three sleeping bodies. In the middle was a tall bearded fellow. His arms and chest were bare, and no doubt the rest of him as well. He was balding but his hair was in a ponytail. He had a lean, handsome face. His left arm lay beneath a young woman who slept facing the wall, her back nestled against the man's rib-cage, her nighty twisted around her torso. It was the French waitress next to her boyfriend, the cook. He slept with his mouth open and his breath clicked through his nostrils as though he were on the verge of a great snore. On his right arm was Gladys. She slept in a white flannel nighty, her lips slightly parted, her face catching little pulses of light from the candle. The cat lay curled and purring at her side. Together they looked not at all like swingers. More like young animals in a litter or kids in an orphanage.

I stood there for a long time, not wanting to wake them, caught in some sort of fascination. So this was how the

other half lived, how they looked after their own. These
people were giving comfort to Gladys. Giving comfort. It
struck me as a rather old-fashioned phrase. Something
painful, something I'd thought long dead, began to proclaim itself in me: a boy lurching through the trees announces to the world that we can be anyone we want to be,
we can be Elvis. Gladys hushes him, holds him upright as
the world spins by. *You only say that, Baby Huey, you only
say that . . . because you're one of those people nothing bad
ever happens to.*

A gauze curtain drifts in from the window by the bed
and floats there, sustained by a rise in the wind. It flutters
over the three sleeping bodies, over the sound of their
breathing, and falls back on to the window.

I lean on the bookcase and something rocks at my elbow.
On the upper shelf, upright, resting against the wall, is my
old ukelele. I hold it up to my ear and ever so lightly
thumb the strings. My . . . dog . . . has . . . fleas. I never
could get the hang of playing the uke very well. I ended up
giving it to Gladys. But now I have the craziest urge to give
these people a concert. Show them I know a thing or two
about having a good time. One for the money, two for the
show, three to get ready, now go cats go. That sort of thing.

They just lie there across that impossible distance
breathing so peacefully, the guy in the middle and one gal
at either side, the shadows jumping on the planes of their
faces. How could he lie there like that, with the French girl
on one arm and Gladys on the other? Surely his arms
would go numb. It doesn't seem to phase him. The ladies
seem as light as angels and he looks for all the world like
their saviour. And this was life on z'etch.

The curtain floats in over the bed again like the ghost of
my youth, the gypsy I wanted to be, the lover, the musician, world traveller, poet, all those aborted selves a man
leaves behind to have a future.

I must have stood there for a long time, long enough for
the candle to start guttering and for time to disappear, and

something like my soul breathing in and out to the sound of their breathing, and then it fell dark in the room. I crept out holding the ukelele. I always meant to send Gladys a note but only now does it occur to me what to say.

The Words of the Juice Woman

"I seen somethin real bad," Winston said softly, but neither of the women seemed to hear him. Lupine Shingoose stared straight ahead, leaning on her massive arms. Her friend Monell hunched over her beer like an old lady and blew smoke up at the ceiling. They had been cursing out men in general and their own absent men in particular. Winston had waited for what felt to be a considerate length of time to tell his news. The women seemed unconnected to his concerns, like the ones whose voices trilled over the P.A. system praising their mountain home in Tennessee in three-part harmony.

Lupine was forty-five, her skin the colour of coffee with a splash of cream. She had a voluptuous mouth, a sturdy mound of a body, and wore her hair in an impressively large beehive. Her friend Monell was younger, a Métis, tall, slim, and seemed to walk away from men's compliments. She had apparently little use for her long black hair and startlingly white teeth. There were too many men in the world. Her own was off fishing with Lupine's ex. They should go fishing more often.

Winston looked around the bar to see if someone might be listening. It was the biggest one he'd ever seen. The bar in Pike Mission would have fit into a single corner of this one. The noise here in the Buckingham was like an indoor rodeo without the horses. He looked back at Lupine and Monell. "Hey," he said softly and banged Lupine's mug several times on the table until she looked at him. "I'm tryin t'tellya somethin." He leaned forward. So did the women, as though anticipating scandal. "Up there on the track, ah? In the stayson. I seen somethin. Toe guys."

Lupine smiled and nudged Monell. "Good lookin?"

"They disagree liddlebit, ah? One guy says human beins come from animals like, the other guy he says they come from God. All I want is to bum a smoke."

"Hey, little brother, you're toe young t'smoke," said Lupine.

"So this guy he's like a preetser, ah? He beats the other guy up liddlebit an I figure it's time I take off for d'hills. But you seen that storm tonight, hey, so me I wait an see."

Monell wanted to know what they looked like.

"Couple a white guys. Couple a real winos," he said.

"So tell us," said Lupine. She wore a look of impatience Winston had come to associate with all older sisters.

"Anyways the other guy he come at this preetser guy with a suvel an really worked him over, ah? The big guy, the preetser guy, he pulls out a knife an I take off."

Both women stared at Winston Shingoose.

"Well, what could a guy do?"

Lupine said, "You could of broughten them guys to the bar. We could of showed em some action, hey Monell?" Both women laughed but Lupine stopped when she saw the look on her brother's face.

"I think mebbe one a them guys bit the dust," he said.

"You seen it happen?" Monell asked.

"I took off."

Lupine turned to her friend. "See what a candy-ass baby brother I got?"

Monell leaned back. Her spine curved and slowly crawled along the seat of her chair. She held her cigarette up in the air and seemed to hide beneath the smoke. "I woulda took off too," she said.

Winston said again, "I think mebbe one a them guys bit the dust. Dar-win, this little guy read Dar-win. That's what he said." He turned to Monell, who also read books. "You hearda this guy Dar-win? Mebbe he wrote a book, ah?"

"Red Darwin?" Monell shook her head and her hair swayed like long grass. "Let's take off," she said.

"Right on, shy gone," he said, because he was nervous in this noisy place.

First he went to the toilet. Again, it was the biggest one he'd ever seen. Men of all ages shuffled slowly past the cubicles or ambled up to the stalls. On the walls of the urinal were mostly swear words and phone numbers. In the cubicles were drawings of parts of people's bodies. The world was a latrine. That's what the little man with the shovel had said. Since everyone came from animals it followed that the whole world was nothing but a mouldy latrine. *There's animals lives in caves, there's some lives in partment blocks. Don't expect nothin more than the slime you come from.* This place was perhaps what the little man had in mind.

Walking back with the women through the empty streets, Winston felt compelled to hurry, but the women took their time, teasing Winston about his northern manner of speech, slipping into his accent, laughing and arguing.

Monell said, "The priest always told us we come from Adam an Eve."

Lupine said, "He was a bullsit artist."

Monell said, "Winston's buddy Darwin, he says we all come from animals."

Winston said, "That's not his name. He's read Darwin."

Lupine said, "Red Darwin is a bullsit artist."

Monell said, "He wrote a book."

Lupine said, "Didn't do him no good, did it." And the women laughed.

Monell said, "My kohkom used to tell us kids we all come from Old Man and Old Woman."

Lupine said, "See's a bullsit artist toe. They're all bullsit artists."

The women laughed until their sides ached, and Winston had to urge them on their way. The streets looked sinister. From time to time a car would race past, muffler screaming, or a drunk would look them over and lurch on by. The whole city seemed an extension of the big latrine inside the Buckingham. The voices of the flabby man with the knife and his little friend seemed almost to whisper in the moonlight through the alleys and parking lots.

Monell said, "This Darwin, he fights with a shovel. I don't trust no guy who fights with a shovel."

Lupine said, "When you bullsit that much you use a suvel for everythin."

The women started laughing again, Winston slumping along behind them, turning his head from time to time to see if they were being followed. The moon hung high and full above the wrecking yards and shacks at the edge of town.

They gave Winston the children's room. It smelled sweet, of puppy breath. Several minutes passed before he could make out the shapes of Lupine's youngest boy on one end of the mattress and a smaller child at the other end. He shut his eyes but he couldn't block out the image of the two men in the abandoned station. They had been sitting on a mattress like this one. They had been drinking. The station smelled of booze and urine. The big flabby one, the one who liked to preach so much, had worn a toque, an old overcoat, and shoes without socks. If he closed his eyes, Winston could see the two of them on their mattress, arguing and yelling. And now the little one was probably dead.

He opened his eyes. He could see better now. There were three children on the mattress. The smallest one must have belonged to Monell. Next to the children was a large cardboard box with a dog in it. She lay with four newborn puppies nestled against her teets. Winston leaned against the wall, naked, wishing he had remembered to get one more cigarette off Monell. He listened to the breathing of the dogs and children. What would be so wrong about coming from animals? Why should that mean the world was nothing but a giant latrine?

He shifted on his mattress. The bitch raised her head into a patch of moonlight and looked straight at Winston. "*Kiskānak,*" he whispered, as though she might change if he didn't name her quickly. Her head and snout were almost too dark to be visible, but her eyes reflected like puddles in the moonlight their cunning look of recognition.

• • •

"And how are you feeling this morning, Mr. Cream?" Miss Parsonage wore a dutiful smile. She stood several feet away from the bed and held her clipboard firmly to her chest.

"I give thanks to the Lord," said Mr. Cream.

"How are those dressings?" she asked, and took two little steps forward.

Mr. Cream considered her question for a moment. "They are a small price to pay for being alive," he said, blinking painfully with his one visible eye.

"That's good," said the girl. "I guess you had a pretty close call."

"There were four of them, my friend. Maybe five. Maybe six. Armed like the savages of days gone by."

Miss Parsonage stood in the centre of the room. Only her eyes moved, scanning the bed and floor for anything out of the ordinary.

"Is my friend Sailor Mulvey . . ."

"Yes, Mr. Cream. I'm sorry. They found him by the tracks."

"Ah," the man sighed, "Sailor was the first to fall." He turned his good eye to the nurse. "We must thank our lucky stars, my friend. We must bury the awful things and look ahead to happier times."

"An investigator wants to speak with you. He said he'd be in later."

"Ah, yes," said Mr. Cream, and closed his one good eye. The other was bandaged.

A woman came in with the juice trolley and Miss Parsonage moved aside. The trolley lumbered up to the bed while Miss Parsonage looked up and down at her watch.

"Ah, yes," said Mr. Cream again, as if rehearsing lines. "There were at least four of them. All Indians. There might have been five. Perhaps six." He squinted at the trolley, lifted up a small glass of apple juice, and closed his eye again. "Some people are throwbacks," he whispered. "They think they come from animals."

"Yes," said Miss Parsonage, and glanced nervously at the woman with the trolley. "So I'll tell the inspector to drop in this afternoon?"

"I know where I came from," said Delbert Cream, "and I will fight any man who fouls that holy place." He sipped his juice.

"Thank you," said Miss Parsonage to the woman.

"Do you know where you came from, my friend?"

"Yes," she said and stood aside to allow the woman to pass with her trolley.

"I have nothing against them, you understand," said Mr. Cream, "but when they leave their reserves behind they should be taught our ways. That they are God's children just as we are."

"*Atimomēy*," said the woman with the trolley, gesturing towards Mr. Cream, and she drew her trolley from the room.

"My-my," said Mr. Cream, his eye open again, "you mean they work in hospitals now?"

God's blessings seem to come as unpredictably as the weather, or so thought Mr. Cream the day the stitches were removed. He had prayed to God for deliverance and was delivered. The same day his stitches came out he told his story about the Unknown Soldier and even that stiff-rumped nurse on dayshift harkened to it. Everyone liked that story. He was given a new suit of clothes – well, almost new – and it looked even more dashing, fit even better than his last. The hospital pastor slipped him a twenty for the road. When the last stitch was out he looked and felt younger than he had in years, and everyone noticed. Stay out of deserted stations, said the doctor. Keep in touch now, said the inspector. *Atimomēy*, said the juice woman with a smile.

"Sweet Jesus," cried Mr. Cream, "make me new again!" and off he strode to the hardware store to prepare for his journey west. A group of Indians lounged along the street. "Make them to understand," he whispered, "make them clean and new like me." His freshly shaven face went all clenched for a moment. "So much animality!" he hissed.

An old gentleman eyeing Mr. Cream looked alarmed. Mr. Cream reached for his toque and said, "Peace, brother," to the old man. In Mr. Cream's hand was a new cloth cap. He stared in confusion at the cap then cried, "Of course!" because his toque had belonged to that other life.

At the hardware store he bought a small hunting knife, and in the washroom of the Buckingham, he hitched up the leg of his trousers and eased the thin blade down into the side of his boot. "There," he said.

• • •

Lupine shoved her face into Winston's line of vision so that he could see nothing else in the bar, not even Monell's lovely hair. She had always been a bossy sister. She could always fix you with her eyes. "You wanna work in this town?" she asked. "It's a tough town for a injun. You wanna drink in this bar, it's tough toe. You don't walk into the Buckingham with your eyes bright an wide. You do that, someone's gonna rearrange your face, hey? Up at the Mission? It's a goddam nursery. This is *tāpwē ispa'yiw*, kid, this here is the real thing."

He looked away, a jumble of words in his head. He wasn't much of a talker.

"You get scared mebbe sometimes?"

He shrugged.

"Everyone from home gets scared down here. Jus' doan let it show."

The waitress returned to their table. "Guy over there bought yiz some beer," she said to Winston and placed three Pilsener on the table.

"Is he good lookin?" said Lupine.

"You must be doin somethin right, Winston," said Monell.

"I wouldn't say he was exactly good lookin," said the waitress.

"Mebbe it's that wimp-assed bastard I got married to," said Lupine, squinting into the crowd.

Ignoring the beer, Winston said, "This town mebbe not such a hot idea."

Monell took a swipe at Winston's cap. He ducked and she missed. She looked him over from one shoulder to the other, examined the silky fabric of his jacket, red with white lettering, on the left arm number ten; on the right, First Base. "This guy's a ten," she said to Lupine. "Hey, number ten, you think you ever get to first base with me?"

He shrugged. She yawned and slumped in her chair. Winston raised his new beer, took a mighty swallow, and closed his eyes. When he opened them, a man was looking down at him, a big man of fifty or more years.

"I believe the name is Winston?" said the man, raising his cap. "And how are you, my friend?"

Winston's throat went dry with the taste of fish hooks and a sharp cramp began to bubble just below his belt.

"May I sit down?" said the man.

"Yer sittin," said Monell, butting her cigarette.

"You've forgotten me, haven't you," said the man. "That's what I said to myself when I saw you with these ladies. I said to myself, 'I'll bet he wouldn't even recognize me.' "

Softly Winston said, "Yuh."

" 'I'll bet,' I said to myself, 'Winston doesn't remember a single thing about me,' " said the man.

"Right on," said Winston.

"You buy this beer?" Monell asked, but the man did not reply.

He kept smiling at Winston. Finally he turned to the women and doffed his cap to each in turn. "Indian Summer," he said. "This is my favourite time of year. Leaves turning, days still warm, sound of geese going over. Makes people in these parts cling to life." He looked up at the smoky ceiling as if searching for words of praise. "Sometimes," he said to Monell, "I just feel like singing thankful hymns."

"*Atimomēy*," said Lupine.

"What?" said the man.

"Dogshit," said Lupine, enunciating with care.

"I beg your pardon?" said the man.

"You can beg my pardon or kiss my ass, Dogshit. You're a real sonofabitch. You know that, Mr. Dogshit? You're a real candy-ass no good bastard. You don't fole me. You maybe fole her but you don't fole me. I been aroun. I seen guys like you. You're a real candy-ass bastard. Why don't you take your beer an go back where you come from? Is this clear what I'm sayin? You stink," said Lupine.

The big man looked suspiciously at the faces before him. His hand crawled like a slug down his leg. Winston saw this and his heart began to churn so loudly he could scarcely hear the exchange of remarks. But even Monell knew now, he could see that. He spotted the rear exit. His legs had never let him down.

The big man seemed to recover. "Once upon a time there was soldier," he said, "and no one knew his name. It could have been Ghandi, Christ, Satan, or Darwin, for all –"

"Fights with a shovel," said Monell. "I don't have no truck with a guy fights with a shovel. Besides, he's tits up, ah?"

The big man looked confused.

Lupine resumed her remarks in her usual monotone, a voice so mechanical it seemed to come from someone else. "You come in here an buy us a beer like you owned us. I know you're jus' a wino. All you want is a fast t'row in the hay with this one, ah?" She jerked her thumb at Monell. "You mebbe fole some people, you don't fole me, hey, Mr. Dogshit. You're a real sonofabitch, you know that? You probly got the clap. I know a sonofabitch when I see one."

The big man's hand resumed its downward voyage. Winston spotted a large glass ashtray in front of Monell, an arm's length away.

The big man smiled right at Lupine, "Haven't we met somewhere?"

"You fleabitten flabbyassed sonofabitch, you get outa here," said Lupine and rose from her table like a bear from a berry patch, a bottle in her left hand.

The big man rose too. Nearly everyone in the bar had turned to look as he drew out his knife and shook it at her. Only the P.A. system could be heard, the same three women praising their mountain home in Tennessee. Delbert took off his cap and made a curious bow, a gesture not entirely insulting, replaced his cap, and took several steps backward. His face was sweating. He didn't seem to know where his knife had come from. He looked like a man who had arrived at the wrong party. They all watched him leave as the noise of chairs and voices returned and men looked away.

"You know that guy?" Monell asked, her eyes round and white-rimmed.

"I seen him a couple of times."

"Who is he?"

"He got some real fancy things to say about people he never met. He said em to the cops. I think mebbe I should of done some work on his teeth."

The waitress turned and said to Winston, "Yiz gonna drink outa that thing or put it back on the table?"

Winston discovered a large ashtray in his hands. He put it back on the table, and when the three women laughed, he blushed.

• • •

As the sun was going down, Delbert Cream sat in the bus station just inside the glass door. His ticket to Saskatoon cost him $9.10, which left him exactly forty-five cents, a small price to pay for an exit from Prince Albert and that bitch with the tongue like a knife. He had twenty minutes before the night bus left, so he could relax and watch the people passing by. You didn't get the same class of people riding the buses these days, that was obvious. There was, however, a nicely dressed lady in the seat next to him. I will close my eyes to the iniquity of this depot, he thought, and pressed the palms of his hands into his eyes. At first he saw the deepest pool of black, then splatters of gold like stars in a dark sky. He relaxed the pressure upon his eyes and thought he saw a shape in the centre, a bear shape. It floated towards him, faster and larger, then went blood red. He looked up, clenching his teeth till his face shook. "The juice woman!" he hissed. "She was the juice woman!" He closed his eyes again and assumed the same position for another look. Presently the shape returned but this time it was a bit smaller, even as it floated closer. "Sailor Mulvey," he said.

"I beg your pardon?" said the woman beside him. She was small and faded and had a very large nose. Her face was nicely made up, her blue and white suit immaculate. "I'm sorry," she said, "but were you saying something to me?"

He turned away from the window to face the woman. As he did so, he failed to see two Indians and a Métis walking by. They were heading home. The young man slouched along with his hands in his pockets. The Métis woman snatched the cap from his head. "w-o-r-t Radio – New Braunfels, Texas," she read. "Where'd you get this?" "A guy I guided," he said. "He tole me I'd be dynamite behind the mike." The third person, a large woman, said, "Oh, you're dynamite all right." The first woman pulled the cap over her long hair.

Delbert Cream turned back to his window, but all he saw was the edge of a massive cloud approaching from the west, blotting out the last rays of the sunset. To the woman beside him he said, "I am troubled in my heart."

"Aw," she crooned.

"Once upon a time," he said, "there was a soldier, and no one knew his name. It could have been Gandhi, it could have been Christ, it could have been Satan or Charlie McCarthy. He fought in the trenches for the Allies. When his gun was empty he fought with a bayonet. And when that was gone, he picked up a pick and shovel and fought with it."

"A pick *and* a shovel?" said the lady.

"Well, I guess it was a pick," he replied. It didn't really matter. What mattered finally was that this man died like a saint; he died swinging that thing until he could swing it no more. He was more than a saint, Delbert ruminated, "He was the only . . . friend I ever . . ."

"Why are you crying?" asked the lady.

"There is so much animality wherever I go!" he whispered.

The woman put on a pair of glasses and inspected Mr. Cream's troubled face for a moment. She couldn't help wondering when the gentleman had last had a good home-cooked meal. "I'm from Saskatoon," she said finally. "It's much nicer there."

The Elevator

Part 1

The Impact of
Contemporary Verse
on Gunnar Held
and Vice Versa

Welcome to English 90, Oral Discourse. My name is Anne
Walker and I am your instructor. This is a non-credit
course sponsored by the University Extension Division. At
the sound of the beep, please tell me your name.

*

This here's Frank Mahovlich.

*

Thank you. These taping sessions will eventually be re-
lated to the course reading material. This first session,
however, will be quite informal. I want you to tell me
about yourself. Several things concern me at this point: Are
you currently in the Spinal Unit or the Re-hab? If you are
still in the Spinal Unit, when do you expect to be residing
in the Re-hab? How did you come to be placed in either of
these places? Perhaps most important, what was your
motivation for taking this course? Please feel at liberty to

talk about yourself. These tapes, I can assure you, are confidential.

*

I'm in the Spinal Unit until they stop diddling with me, then I'll be in the Re-hab with all the other gimps. I'll let you guess how come I'm taking this course. As to how I come here, that's quite a story.

While back we had a game in Saskatoon. Those buggers was no slouches and for once we had to hustle our butts. Me and this guy, we been matched up all night. He was big and fast, like a frigging shadow. Second period I'd had enough, eh, so I come in and blindsided him. It was a pretty clean check, it knocked the wind out of him and he missed a few shifts. We tied the game up and I'm starting to feel real loose out there. Third period he's back again, I guess he must of been gunning for me. I was chasing the puck into the corner and I had a stride on him. So he comes up behind me just as I get to the puck, and my head's still down, eh? Then he rams me into the boards and something snaps. Down I go, I can't feel nothing. Last thing I remember, Old Doc Wheels is coming after me in her wheelchair. Did I dream that part about her? I guess.

Maybe you know her, eh?

Anyways, I wake up in the hospital with a broken neck, your fourth cervical vertebrae, that's what this Jap doctor says. Partial lesion of the spine, etc., etc. Bunch of doctors hemming and hawing about this and that. I can talk and work this here tape, my head's okay. I can even shrug my shoulders a little, but that's all I got. I mean even though I can get took places in the hospital in a wheelchair, my head's all I got, I don't feel nothing below. I'm a goddam head without a body.

Last week a bunch of doctors come and said I could maybe some day get a operation. But this here Jap doctor he says no way. He's the only one levels with me - hang on . . . you fuck off, nurse. I'm still talkin here! - he's the only

one levels with me so I guess that's it. She's a tits-up propo-
sition.

I get visitors now and then, I mean besides that fat-assed
head nurse. My old man he just more or less sits there, he
never was much for conversation. He keeps saying they
should of give me a colour set, this here black and white's
not up to much. I could give a good goddam.

Sometimes Debbie Johanesson brings me books. Once
she and my old man come together, tried to cheer me up.
She shaved me, give me a haircut. Likely she's got a boyfriend somewheres. I don't ask.

I been getting a lot of bad news lately, as if I didn't have
enough. It's made me think hard on things. It's made me
change my mind on some of them. For instance, I been
thinking about how Doc Wheels come at me in her wheelchair with her hands out and I took off. Maybe you know
who I'm talking about now, eh? Maybe it wasn't the first
time I done that, took off on someone. When Charlotte was
knocked up I told her, go get rid of it, it's only a egg, I says.
I'll pay for getting it done. But oh no, she went and had the
kid, so I hit the road. And after she give it up I started
going with her again. It wasn't my kid, we both knew it
wasn't my kid. She didn't say whose and I never asked.
Some bozo back home, I figure.

Nothing was ever quite right after that. She was more or
less, you might say, not in the mood and anyways I had this
thing on the side with Debbie Johanesson. Great while it
lasted. Sometimes she'd even wake me up in the middle of
the night for a poke.

I'm getting off the topic. Back home the teachers always
said I could never keep to the topic.

It never rains but it pisses, eh? The head nurse comes in
last week, starts to bitch and moan, says I'm not taking my
pills and I'm not eating nothing. Eat up, she says. I tells
her, the slop they feed us in here would make a preacher
swear. I knocked this custard on the floor with my chin.
She says I got no respect or appreciation – like all along

she's been doing me some kind of favour. I tells her to go ride the nearest doorknob. She tells me either I eat up or I can't watch the playoffs. I says to her, you can always tell who the head nurse is in here. She's the one with scabs on her knees.

I never could keep my temper. I done it to myself again. She got my television. The only time I might of wanted it. Probably this'll be the time Toronto takes it all. I told her, either she brings that sucker back or I'll go on a hunger strike. That's where it stands.

I been thinking about that night in the elevator last year. I should of minded my tongue. I mean Doc Wheels. I should of listened better, shouldn't of took off. I should of took her by the hands, held hands with her. Because if I had of done that, then maybe she'd get the notion to come over here and maybe we could chew the rag a bit.

I guess by now you know who I'm talking about. What I mean to say is, you're the only person could understand what I been through. And if you wanted to open up and get personal, even talk about sex and things like that, I'd listen. I got nothing pressing, I got nowheres to go. Hell, we could talk all night. Piss on the head nurse.

I just listened to my voice on the tape. I wish I could use this here erase button. I never knew I could be such a candy-ass. I didn't even say what I meant to say. It's this frigging placater, I can't get used to it. Working a tape machine with a placater is about as easy as stickhandling with your hands tied. You paraplegics think you got it tough, eh? You should try working a tape machine with a frigging placater some day.

*

Mr. Mahovlich? Apparently we've met. In fact, I do recall the incident by the elevator of the Arts Building more than a year ago. And if I'm not mistaken, a Miss Johanesson approached me last month regarding you and your . . . ah

. . . . With regard to your request, Mr. Mahovlich, I'm afraid my schedule on and off campus does not permit many individual visits at this time. However, when I have some breathing space during the summer recess, perhaps I will have the time. In the meantime you'll have to try to cope with the course as best you can. It can be therapeutic in the long run if you apply yourself. I'm assuming you *do* want to take this course. If so, it may seem bewildering at first. I sympathize with you on the matter of your applicator. It will seem awkward for a while. Some patients tell me the wooden ones are best because they feel less abrasive in the mouth.

One bothersome point. I can't find a Frank Mahovlich on my course list. Have you been properly registered? If not, one of the nurses can fill out the required forms. Let me know if you still have these forms and if the texts for this course have arrived. I'm assuming that by next week you will begin responding to the texts. In the meantime, if you would like to speak about something familiar to you, a hockey anecdote, for instance, I would be glad to comment on your style of delivery. Your account of your accident was interesting. And this incident where we met, I'm intrigued that you remembered . . . well . . . remembered those details. Perhaps you could talk more about this incident in the elevator.

Your use of the persona "Doc Wheels" suggests a tack for future discourse. I want you to avoid referring to me in the second . . . with reference to that night. Keep all personal references in the third person. *She* did this, *she* said that, etc.

Good luck on your next piece, Mr. Mahovlich.

*

I was putting you on about my name. It was like a joke, eh? I'm Gunnar Held. I figured you'd remember.

I haven't gotten around to them books yet, so if it's okay by you I'm going for the personal antidote stuff. I thought

I'd start with this here thing happened to me way last year.
It was no big deal then but it keeps coming back to me, so I
guess it must of been important. That's the time I met Doc
Wheels. I can remember most of what she said and how she
talked then. I can even do a half-decent takeoff on her.
Hey, Doc Wheels, what do you think about that? You
listen good, eh?

This here happened in February. I know it was February because the season was winding down and we only had
to win maybe two or three more to have first place all sewed
up. We had a good team.

Stick to the topic, Gunnar, stick to the topic, right?
Well, here goes nothing.

I was in Saskatoon on the campus Friday night and
things there had mostly shut down. Except for the bar.
Makes you wonder when them so-called "scholars" does
any studying. I was in what they called the Arts Building. I
had to deliver something for Charlotte on account of she
was laid up with the flu. Her prof give her till Saturday. All
I had to do was shove it under his door.

The office was up on the tenth floor so I took the elevator,
naturally, which turned out to be like a very big mistake.
Her prof was a guy named Goplin. He taught something
called "The Family" or "Family Life," and she was always
raving about him. I used to have this idea maybe she had
the hots for him. Then one day I met him and seen what a
sawed-off little pecker he was. All nose and no chin to
speak of and more than a bit light on his feet, if you catch
my drift. I had to wonder what she seen in him, right? And
the subject, Family Life, I mean give me a break. If you
lived in a family like most people, why for chrissakes
should you have to study it? Maybe if you was a orphan or
something like that, it might make sense. Once I says to
her, I says, "Family Life is what you hang on to if you
wear a can on the ice." Didn't even crack a smile. The way
I figure it, the more education you give a woman the less
chance she's got of coming out the other end with a sense

of humour. You *need* a sense of humour, it's goddam gloomy enough in this life without one I'll tell the world. I know, stick to the topic.

Anyways, I shove Charlotte's assignment under Goplin's door, I gets into the elevator, and down she goes. I remember looking at the numbers: ten, nine, eight, seven, six, five . . . it was a very slow elevator. When I get down past the fifth, out go the lights and she creaks to a stop.

Well holy baldheaded, I says to myself, this is really my night, eh? You try to help someone out and where does it land you? I mean I didn't have to deliver that jerkoff assignment for Charlotte. I could of gone drinking, maybe took in a movie. Even paid a visit to Debbie Johanesson. But oh no, here's old Gunnar between the fourth and fifth floor in this jerkoff elevator blacker than the inside of a bruised crow. I mean, you dream of situations when you're in a elevator with some woman and the lights go out, eh? And you're stuck there with nothing to do? You maybe shoot the shit for a while and then light a match and sort of check her out? And wow, she's real Canada Fancy all the way, great set of kazongas. And she's all of a sudden real hot for it? Well, not this time, folks. Old Gunnar, he really knows how to pick a elevator.

Hey, I hope I'm not getting too personal for you, Doc. You said don't hold nothing back, right?

It was dark in that there elevator, I mean like very dark. I lit my lighter and found the buttons and pushed the emergency one. It was maybe the only thing that worked in that goddam building. Typical government operation if you ask me. I ring and ring but no dice. I notice this little metal door where the telephone's supposed to be, some bozo'd gone and ripped it out. Nothing but a handful of wires. I'm starting to think maybe somebody up there's trying to get back at me for too many elbows in the corners or something. I get touchy when I'm holed up. I've never been real wild about closets and small rooms.

Anyways, I'm hunkered down holding my lighter with

one hand and counting my smokes with the other. I had eleven, I can remember to this day. Then I hears this noise above my head, it's like metal clanking and something going by, maybe a janitor's cart or something. I starts to holler and ring the bell again. And after a while I hear this woman's voice, like very faint. "Are you all right down there?" she says.

Maybe the only thing I done right that whole night was I gets out my penknife and finds the crack between the doors and goes to it with the blade. Pretty soon the doors are split enough so's I can get my fingers in and pull like hell. One thing, I'm strong, eh, and twice as strong when I'm mad. So pretty soon I gets the doors open maybe half a inch. That's all, she won't budge no more. I seen nothing but darkness through the crack. Then this little mousy voice from above says, "There's been a power failure. This part of the city's in total darkness."

"Great," I says. "Just great."

"I don't even have a flashlight," she says.

So while I'm throwing a small conniption in there she takes off. Before I know it she's back with a candle, a long skinny candle. Can you believe it? She shoves it through the crack in the doors. "Where'd you get that?" I says.

"In my office," she says.

I ask her what she's doing in a office at that time of night and she tells me she's a prof of some kind. If she ever finishes her thesis she gets to be a doctor, another Goplin for God's sake, and she wasn't much older than Charlotte. (Eh, Doc? I'd put you at just shy of thirty. What do you say?)

Anyways, where was I? Oh, yeah. I lights up this here candle and hey boys, let me tell you, was I ever glad. You never appreciate seeing till you been blind, eh? I'm really getting off on this here candle when Doc Wheels she hollers down something about, could she get me anything else, a package of soda biscuits or a book or something.

I says, "I want outa here."

She says, "The maintenance people don't answer."

I says, "Well, would you mind rousting them up?"

She says, "They're probably busy. This is an emergency."

"So is this," I says. "You think I got nothing better to do than fart around in this hole?"

She says, "We'll just have to wait. You'll have to be patient."

I starts to thinking, she give me a candle, right, it's maybe eleven o'clock Friday night, she clanks around in the hallway like maybe she wears chains or something, and she calls herself a prof? So I ask her real calm, I says, "You keep kinda late hours, dontcha?"

She says, "I'm grading papers."

"On a Friday night?"

"The whole weekend," she says.

"Don't you never go home?"

"Sometimes I mark at night," she says, funnylike, as if she doesn't want to admit nothing. "I can concentrate better. Are you sure I can't get you something to read?"

"Whatcha got?"

"Do you read novels?"

"Like what?"

"I'll see," she says and off she goes, clankety-clank. She comes back with a saucer for the candle and a book. The book's too thick for the crack. So she gives me the saucer and goes back for another try.

"This one won't fit either," she says, like she figures I'm going to be heartbroken that I couldn't read it.

I try being polite. I says, "Maybe you could try the maintenance again."

"I just did," she says. "Still no answer."

"What about the fire department?"

"Oh, I really doubt –"

"Well *try* them, for God's sake! You think I want to hibernate in here?"

She sighs real loud so's I get the full benefit, and off she goes clankety-clank. I don't go around throwing a shit-fit every day of the week, but sometimes you gotta let them know you mean business, otherwise they'll treat you like dirt. I expect the better part of the campus is like that, they think just because they're educated they can treat people like they crawled out of a garbage can. That's their major problem.

"I can't get through," she says. "Half the city must be phoning in. I'm afraid you'll just have to sit tight."

Well, what do you do, eh? I lay down and have a smoke. After a while I hear something up there, sounds like someone breathing hard.

"Is that you?" I says.

"Is *what* me?"

"Are you into heavy breathing or something?" I figures she might laugh but no way. Another laugh-a-minute number, this university's full of them. Then I thought, shit, maybe she really *is* into heavy breathing. Waits for elevators to go on the fritz so's she can breathe on people. It give me the weirdest feeling.

"Hey," I says, "I was only joking."

She just keeps on breathing, not a peep otherwise. Then she ups and clanks down the hall. I light another smoke and a while later she's back.

"I want my candle," she says.

"Come and get it," I says.

"I've got better things to do than sit in the dark up here."

"Try standing. Take a load off your mind."

No answer.

"Just tell me one thing," I says. "Are you some kind of night janitor?"

"I told you. I'm a sessional instructor."

"Then if you're a instructor, why d'you go everywhere with a janitor's cart?"

She gets real sarcastic, says something about in case I

thought I was another Sherlock Holmes, like forget it. Deduction ain't my strong suit. Old Doc Wheels has a real sharp tongue, seems to me.

"Then what's all that clanking?" I says.

"I happen to move in a wheelchair."

Jesus H. Christ, what do you say, eh? I nearly shit. Well, hell, I try to soft-soap her but no way with this one. I tells her, "Look," I says, "how was I to know?"

"Next time," she says, "you might try asking."

"So I made a mistake. What makes you so touchy?"

"What makes you so presumptuous?" That's the word she used. That's it, I says to myself, she's sensitive about being a gimp. That's her major problem.

What do you think, Doc? Am I knocking on the door, eh?

A while later I says, "Look, you can have your candle. I don't need it no more." I blow it out to show her I mean what I say. But she doesn't say nothing. I figure she's still sore.

I've always sort of had this tendency towards losing my temper. When something doesn't work or someone's jacking me around I blow up. I just can't help it until maybe I've popped someone or said something I shouldn't of. My old man says I got a real problem. He should talk. I'm not like some guys. I don't go slinking around hiding things or carrying grudges. Once I make my little scene I settle right down again all smiles. I miss playing hockey. You don't let nothing build up. A guy gets chippy, you take him into the boards or you drop the gloves. Hell, chances are when the season's over, you meet the guy in the bar, you're the best of buddies. That happened to me with Arch. Best friend I ever had. It all started with a elbow in the teeth. I know, Doc. Archie Willens isn't your favourite person.

Anyways, you – I mean she – takes off down the hall and I know I've gone and pissed her off. I starts thinking about my temper. I shouldn't of blown up at her like that. If I'd of known she was a invalid I know I would of went easier on her. You got to treat invalids with kid gloves. So I sits there feeling pissed off at myself. It was like a game misconduct, except in the dark. I didn't even hear her when she come back. All of a sudden there's this crabby little voice saying, "The city fire department does not consider our case an emergency and Maintenance still does not answer."

"What do you mean 'our case'?"

"Has it not occurred to you that I too am stuck here until the elevators are going again?"

"Still sore, eh?"

"No, I'm just trying to explain."

"Well, I guess I lost my cool down here. I mean it's not every day I get stuck in a frigging elevator, scuse my French."

"Why did you blow out the candle?"

"I was gonna give it back."

"It doesn't matter. I can still use the phone without it. I have matches. You should light the candle. It's special, it was a gift to me."

So I lights her up again. "There," she says, "I can see it too." It turns out the top three or four feet of the elevator's even with the fifth floor, so she's looking down on me from up there on her floor.

"About them books," I says, "you got anything smaller?" I only says this to get back on her good side. I figure if I offer to read her books she'll think I'm halfway civilized. I got nothing against reading books. These days I do a fair bit. Maybe she started something, you never know.

Hey Doc. You think you started something, eh?

Anyways, the reason I wanted to get back on her good side was I had to piss like a racehorse. Charlotte give me a couple of beers so's I'd take her assignment over to Goplin's office. Then I had a couple at the bar on campus. I shouldn't of. I might of lasted the whole night. So I figured if I got her on my side, I mean Doc Wheels up there, she'd keep phoning and get me out before too long. Nothing worse than having to piss and nowheres to go.

After a bit, she shoves a skinny book through the crack, it's a bunch of poems. "Poems?" I says. "I don't want to read no poems."

"These are the only slim volumes I have."

Slim volumes, she calls them. Horseshit, I calls them. They're by a guy, name escapes me, he sends his words high and low all over the page. Some of the words don't make no sense, sometimes he just runs a bunch of words together, you come to the end of the poem and think what the hell was that. A kid could of wrote this. He's got this balloon man who gets off on kids, and people living in this here "how town." I didn't want to sound dippy so I says, "You got anything that rhymes?"

She's got a whole pile of books up there. She fires down another skinny one by a woman, her name escapes me too. She wrote about her old man, really calls him down, daddy this and daddy that. He's a bastard and a Nazi and a vampire and that's not the half of it. Turns out she's already killed the old fart. I mean if he's already dead and she killed him, why's she still killing him and still talking to him? I figure this author was crazy as a cut calf.

I wanted to tell Doc Wheels I had to piss real bad, and to phone the maintenance again. But I figured I could maybe last another half-hour. Besides, how do you tell a broad like that you have to take a leak? I mean she just sits there in the dark while I'm reading this crap, she makes me kind of nervous, you see what I mean? So all I says is, "You got anything with some action to it?" She hands me this thing by a guy writes poems about the sea. Real long-winded. I found one where this whale gets in a fight with a kraken and eats it. Turns out a kraken's just a fancy name for a big octopus. But this guy's a poet, eh, and so he doesn't come out and *say* this here's just a big octopus. You can tell I'm really big on poetry, right? Anyways, that was okay. He could of said it in half the space but it was good action all the way. I remember one line, it goes,

> *Tail and skull and teeth and maw*
> *Met sinew, cartilage and claw.*

Ten times better than that woman. Sylvia Pratt, that was her name.

She give me some more and I tried a few. Mostly a foreign language, if you ask me. I found some horny ones too. One by a guy supposed to be a Canadian. In fact most of the ones she give me was Canadians on account of their books was skinniest. That's what she says. I never heard of none of them.

In one of them this dude says something about, You got the lovers, eh. You got the lovers. They're all tangled up in each other's hair feeling each other up, feeling good, eh. Made me think of Debbie Johanesson and then Charlotte and then maybe both of them and me in the same bed. I started getting all hot and bothered, made me have to piss twice as bad, and I started to feel like a goddam peeping Tom. It was the poem done it.

And dirty? There's so much plain dirt passes for poetry you wonder how these bozos got by the censors. I mean this one poet he wants the guys reading him to feel like they just got their dick chopped off and then – I would not even repeat what he says ought to be done with it. I says to old Doc Wheels up there, I says, "This here's the squirreliest stuff I ever read in my life."

"You must mean Irving Layton," she says.

"No," I says, "the whole shitteroo. These here authors, they all belong on the funny farm."

"Well, perhaps your taste isn't terribly modern. I mean some of those poems are a bit . . . off the wall, but there are some nice love poems and –"

"Love poems! One woman's drivin spikes through her old man's chest, one guy invites in the neighbours to watch him and his girl go to it, here's this Mexican woman doin it with a donkey, I mean whatever happened t'the roses that bloom in the spring tra-la, eh?"

Well, wouldn't you know it, she starts laughing, and that really honks me off. Here she is, she can skip up and down the fifth floor with her little books or do anything she bloody well pleases and I'm under her thumb. If she feels like doing the heavy breathing, I gotta go along with it. If she chooses to give me books by a bunch of sickos, I gotta read them. No way I'm gonna tell her I have to pee, she'd just use it to her advantage. That's what Charlotte calls doing a head trip on someone. First time I ever realized what that expression meant. This woman's doing a head trip on me. Only one thing to do. One by one I up and shoves those poetry books back out through the crack.

"What are you doing? You'll rip the jackets."

"Be thankful I didn't rip them books from earhole to arsehole."

"But you asked –"

"I didn't ask for junk to read and I didn't ask to be made a fool of." What I didn't tell her was them books give me the creeps. There's a lot of things I'm not afraid of but reading sicko poetry in a goddam stuck elevator by candle-light is not my idea of a good time. Like Arch says, I'd rather slide down a razor blade.

"I'm sorry. It's just . . . you have a way with words."

I don't know about women. Sometimes they don't laugh when you crack a joke but they do laugh when you say something that's not funny. Charlotte does this all the time. Never used to be like that neither. Not till she come to this here "institute of higher learning." Guys like Goplin pussyfooting around. I says to Doc Wheels, I says, "You're a regular barrel of laughs yourself."

"My name is Anne. What's yours?"

"I'm Gunnar."

"Well, Gunnar, it looks like we're stuck here in the dark for a while." She goes on about this and that, tries to get me talking about myself. I'm still not so sure about her so I don't say much. All's I can think of is, if I don't siphon the python real soon I'm going to have a busted bladder on my hands. I mean it's beyond being funny by now, eh? It's like someone was inflating a basketball inside my guts. Hardly any room left for breathing.

Made me wonder what it's like to be a invalid. I up and ask her, what's it like to be in a wheelchair and all that. She tells me she's been in that contraption since she was fourteen and there's no way she'll ever get out of it neither. She got some kind of disease, name escapes me. It more or less what you might say froze her from the waist down, got part of one arm and not the other, got to her lungs too, that's why she breathes so loud. I felt kind of stupid when she told me that. I switches the topic.

"Do you like them books of poetry. I mean really *like* them?"

"Yes. Of course."

"Well, you can have em. Me, when I read something, I want it straight from the hip. None of this head trip B.S."

"Give me an example."

I had to think for a bit, got my mind off having to take a leak. Then it come to me. "That there guy wrote 'Whose Woods These Are Y'think I'd Know.' "

"Robert Frost?"

"That's the fellow," I says, then I spout off a line or two. Teacher back home in Togo, she made us learn the whole thing. It never turned me on at the time but it come in handy now. I figure if I'm going to win this here argument I got to play Doc Wheels in her own arena.

> *Whose woods these are y'think I'd know*
> *His house is in the village, so*
> *I thought I'd somethin somethin here*
> *An watch his woods fill up with snow.*

Now that's something a person can relate to. Stopping to see something nice, eh? The horse gets antsie because he knows no one stops on the road when there's no farmhouse nearby. Then the guy takes off because he's going somewheres. Like the guy says he's got promises to keep. You can *relate* to that. So I tell her that, quotes and all.

"It's a nice poem," she says.

"Well, why didn't you give me some Robert Frost instead a these here closet cases?"

"Frost's *Collected Poems* is too thick a volume. It wouldn't fit."

"Well, sonofabitch, eh? Then we agree on something. Now don't get me wrong," I says. "I mean maybe that other crap's got hidden meanings and maybe if I was doin a course on the stuff I'd learn all about how to read meanings into things and all that, but for the most part I'd say this modern stuff's pretty shaky. Let me ask a question, okay? No guff now. Are you a atheist? You don't have to worry about sayin you are one, I mean I haven't seen the inside of a church since I got baptized, but I bet you're a atheist, right?"

"I'm a Christian," she says. Just like that: I'm a Christian.

"You call yourself a Christian and you read shit like that? Scuse my French."

"I have a . . . wavering faith, I struggle with doubt, but yes, I'm a Christian."

"Coulda fooled me."

"Those books you dislike . . ." she says, and she stops and thinks for a bit, "they help me to see things through other people's eyes. They help me to feel other people's pain, and other emotions as well. They help me to make some sense out of this world. You must admit, it's a confusing world."

"Not till now it wasn't."

"But does this make sense to you?"

"Yeah . . . well, it's a free country." By this time, like Arch says, my back teeth was floating. She goes on and on about poetry, and all I can think of is when and where and how and that sort of thing. Finally I just cut her off.

"Scuse me, Miss? Scuse me, but I'm sorry. I gotta take a leak."

"What?"

"I said, I gotta take a leak. I mean I gotta take a leak so bad, if I don't do it soon, I don't know what I'm gonna do. I mean if I don't take a leak in five minutes I'm gonna bust, it's that bad. Don't mind me for interrupting you, eh, but could you please phone the fucking maintenance please? I'd appreciate it."

"Oh, my God, why didn't you *say* something?" And off she goes down the hall. I tell her to hurry but I doubt she heard me. I start pacing around wondering if I could stick it through the crack and piss down the shaft so's it wouldn't stink up the elevator. I mean I am like in *pain*. If I wait any longer I get the feeling I'll be all swole up like Charlotte back home when she was knocked up. I know, stick to the topic, etc., etc.

"Gunnar?"

It's Doc Wheels and she's got some good news and some bad news. That's how she puts it. When you're in pain you find out everybody's a goddam comedian.

"The bad news is that Maintenance is tied up until the morning shift comes on. The good news is this!" She hands me – you won't believe this – she hands me this here thing like a plastic flask? She wears it on her leg, calls it her kipper. This one's her spare. Never travels nowheres without a spare. She hands me this thing and says go to her.

Now this may sound weird, but once I got going and I could feel the relief, I mean just the pure relief, I started thinking maybe this Anne woman's not such a bad broad after all. I mean, when you think about it, she give me this here kipper when she maybe might of needed it herself later. That happens, eh? Sometimes you get caught short. And here this Anne woman she shoves her kipper through the crack and says go *to* her. It's the strangest thing.

It's like life, you know? Hell, old Arch give me a elbow

in the chops and I drop my gloves and plough him one and he ploughs me one and we're down on the ice just a-kicking and a-gouging away, the next time I run into him it's like we was brothers. Hockey season he's my enemy, springtime he's my friend. I don't care what you said back then, Doc, I miss old Arch.

And now this. One minute I'm in a goddam tomb at the mercy of this sadistic gimp of a female prof, I piss into her kipper and bingo, we're the best of friends. It makes you wonder.

Hey, Doc, how'm I doing? You like that last bit, eh? Bet you think I like talking into this contraption. Bet you think I'll never stop. Well, you better listen, cause you're the star of this show. I bet you didn't know I had such a good memory, eh? You just listen, I'll give you memory. Like they say on the television, this here's your life.

I know, Doc. I'm breaking the rules. None of this here person-to-person crap. Too much like fraternizing. You like that word, Doc? You better like it. You taught it to me. I know, I'm breaking the rules. Just thought I'd say hi. Don't give me no "F" on the final, eh?

One more thing. I seen the books we gotta read for this here course. Do you mind if I skip the poetry?

*

Mr. Held, let me begin by saying that your anecdote was ... extremely diverting. I played it back twice. To quote your persona, Doc Wheels, "You have a way with words." I hope this does not sound patronizing. I mean it sincerely.

But perhaps it's time you realized that you have joined the ranks of the quadriplegics, just as I am in the ranks of the wheelchair-impaired. Surely terms such as "gimp" and "invalid" can be discarded. Do you see yourself as a gimp? I sincerely hope not. We are whole as human beings, and as such entitled to be described as nothing less than human. I must admit to a personal loathing for the term "invalid." It seems to imply that as human beings we are in*valid*. Perhaps, as well, you ought to think about your attitude to men who are something less than macho. I am referring here to Professor Goplin, whom I know. His sexual orientation is none of my business, but if he is – or any man is – gay, is this any reason to classify him as a freak? I think not, Mr. Held.

On to better things. Since you've had the books all along, and since poetry is (still) not to your liking, I suggest that you begin with J.D. Salinger's *The Catcher in the Rye*. It's very readable. I'm hoping to get your ongoing personal reaction to these books, so tell me what you think about Holden Caulfield. For instance, do you think he is dealing realistically with the world around him?

Good luck, Mr. Held.

*

Hi, teach. What's shaking? I'm a bit bogged down on this here Caulfield book. Every time a nurse starts turning pages for me I get pissed off. For one thing, the guy's a kid and what's a kid supposed to be able to tell me about life, eh? For another thing, he does a hell of a lot of bitching, and he don't even do it grammatical. Haw, haw, you're busting a gut, right? Old Gunnar should talk. But you could do ten times better, Doc. You know them rules. I'm no expert on grammar or nothing, but at least I can fake it if I'm halfways inclined to. I figure this Salinger's definitely in the minor leagues. If a guy can't write he can't write, right?

Anyways, I'm going to talk along the human interest line again, eh? I mean if it's okay by you. No one in this place wants to know what's on your mind. And let's face it, if something's on your mind it's a damn sight easier telling it to a machine than to a real person. Besides, I think you've got a better chance of getting my drift than some little nurse who's never been a gimp in her life, eh? I mean a wheelchair-impaired.

Anyways, as you know, our story isn't finished because after we was settling in for a night of it, you told me the *real* reason you was in that building. Remember? That guy Thorn up and died, right? And face it, Doc, you was in pretty rough – Hang on, it's Charlotte.

It's me again. Charlotte come in. You might say we had words. She was getting all gloomy, just when I was beginning to feel good about this here course. Going on and on about how she should of maybe kept the kid. She's got no idea who has him. She says she keeps having dreams about him. This here kid's always lost and calling for her.

"So what?" I says. "If you had a kid you couldn't afford no university. You couldn't study the family. You couldn't have no seminars with that looker Goplin." No offence to Goplin, you understand, Doc. I mean if a guy wants to be a flit that's his business.

Well, before long, Charlotte announces she's going out with some bozo. I says, who, Goplin? She says no, it's not Goplin. Guess again, it's a old friend of ours. I wasn't in the mood for no Front Page Challenge, so I says out with it, and she says the one word guaranteed to drive me around the bend.

"Archie."

That Charlotte. She always had a eye for the jugular. Could be she was aiming a little lower than that.

I figure this here Holden Caulfield is living in the past. You can't live in the past and hope to get anywheres. That's what I figure.

Hey, Doc. Remember when you told me the real reason you was in that building so late on a Friday night? Eh?

Jesus, there I go again. Breaking the rules. Well, Doc, it's too hard to erase things on this sucker with a goddam placater, so tough shit. I'm starting over.

I remember when Doc Wheels told me the real reason

she was in that building so late at night. She was there for
the whole weekend. Packed her lunch, the whole bit. Turns
out some prof's just up and died and Doc Wheels, she's
having herself like a private wake? Weird, right?

"We're all rather numbed by the thing," she says. "He was
only sixty-four. He could have taught for two or three more
years. They would have let him. His mind was younger and
more alive than most men's thirty years younger."

"Who's 'we'?" I says.

"The whole department," she says. "There's this enormous gulf in his absence. We all feel it. Secretaries, grad
students, even his political enemies."

I still didn't get it. I wanted to ask what she was doing in
the building. I mean this guy was dead, right? But I didn't
have no way of saying it. After a while she goes on, she
says, "You'll think I'm completely mad, but when I saw
the lights go out, and a few minutes later heard you shout-
ing and ringing away in the elevator . . . I thought for a
moment . . . well . . . that it was him!"

"No shit."

"I know that sounds insane, I know it does. It's just . . .
that man had such . . . presence here." She's up there
flipping pages, I can hear. Maybe it's the dark making her
nervous. "You don't mind my going on like this, do you?"
she says.

"Beats readin them poems all t'hell."

"Have you ever lost someone close?" she says.

I says, "Nope," but now I think about it, that wasn't
quite true, Doc. The old lady croaked when I was nine or
ten but I didn't say nothing about that. For one thing, I
didn't remember much. All's I could remember was the
shit we went through with my old man after she croaked.
But I didn't say nothing.

I used to feel funny bellyaching about something that's
gone and done with. Now I think about it, though, I guess
there's worse things.

Anyways, you asked me – she asks me a question. She

says, "Do you remember I told you I had struggled with doubt?"

I says, "Run that by me again?"

"I mean with my faith," she says.

Turns out this Thorn guy's death is the reason for it. Him dying young and all that. (She figures sixty-four is pretty young. I didn't tell her no different.) It's the lousiness of it all, that's the word she used. She was sort of babbling. She said it like the guy's ghost was right there in the building. Then she starts moaning about him being the thing that always held her up, kept her going over the last seven years. Having him up there on the fifth floor, she says, it give her something to believe in. "When he died, my scaffolding just caved in." Scaffolding. That's the word she used.

Every time someone starts to piss and moan like that, Doc, I just spout off what the old man told me. He always says, "If it hurts, don't let it show." This time I didn't say it though. I couldn't just put you down, I mean her down, so I says something like, that's the way she goes. I think I even maybe called her by her first name. Jesus, it was a long night. Pretty soon she starts telling me some of the gory details, eh. It was cancer, and he come to class and everybody knew he was dying, etc., etc.

"It would just break your heart," she says, just like that: it would just break your heart. One day he was lecturing in one of them big amphitheatres, reading from something. He starts clearing his throat. He's had this here cheemotherapy and some of it got done to his throat. So the more the guy talked the more he had to clear his throat, and the more he had to clear his throat, the more it hurt, right? Finally he starts to cough, and jeez it's like the guy's choking to death.

"And do you know what he said?" she says to me. "Do you know what he said?"

Tell the truth, I could of cared less. Jesus H. Christ I wanted out of there.

Well, apparently this Thorn guy, he's up there in front of fifty students or more and he says something about shuffling off his mortal coil, eh, which made like a lot of sense to me. What he meant was, like, to die. Why don't I just shuffle off and die and be done with it? That's basically what he said in front of all them students.

"We were all just stunned. No one said a thing. I just wanted to put my arms around him," she says.

Well, she goes *on* and *on*. She goes into the final stages of the guy's death, eh, and she gets to the part where he's in a ward, some kind of semi-private with one other guy. Turns out this happened about two months before me and Doc Wheels had our all-nighter.

"It was terminal, we all knew it," she says. But they was all hoping he might have what she calls a remission, eh, where it stops eating him up for a while. No way. "He would never leave the hospital," she says. "He would die there." Then old Doc Wheels, she goes into high gear. "Well!" she says. "You'd think that hospital just might have tried to make his last days bearable, wouldn't you? I mean wouldn't you? Do you know who they put him in with?"

"Nope."

She uses this word I never heard before, means cave man. "This Neanderthal with a radio who had not one ounce of sympathy in him. Not one ounce. Day and night he would play the radio and the television. Sometimes he'd even play them both at the same time."

I had to wonder, doesn't everybody do that once in a while? But I never said nothing. Turns out the guy with the radio, he never played no long-hair and that's the only thing this here Thorn guy ever liked.

"This . . . this slob . . . never changed the station once. Day in and day out it was mindless radio commercials about where to get the best deals on wallpaper or station wagons and blaring pop music. You know the kind," she says to me. "These infantile voices singing through their noses. Or on the television it was sitcoms and quiz shows. I mean this is a man who lived his life with . . ." Blahblah and blahblah. She mentions some long-hair musicians, foreign names, naturally. I don't remember who-all.

"Thorn was helpless," she says. "He asked this man, 'Would you please turn it down?' "

"What station was it?" I says.

"Oh, I don't know," she says. "Those teenybopper stations, they're all the same. Just one commercial after another."

A lot she knows about it. "Me, I don't mind commercials so much," I says. "I just tune em out in my head."

Well, you'd think I just said, "Hey, let's go shoot the Pope." She up and tells me how I wasn't none too sensitive to language. She has a whole lot to say about that. How on the TV and radio the language gets such a shit kicking. This guy Thorn, he was like her. He couldn't stand that.

"You must admit," she says to me, "that if your radio was persecuting somebody, you'd at least turn it down, wouldn't you? I mean this big cretin was not confined to his bed. He could have gone out to the lounge to watch television." I remember that perfectly. This cave man, now he's a cretin and his radio's persecuting people. I get the impression after a while me and her we don't exactly see eye to eye on people, you might say.

"He was lucky," she says. She's still going on about this guy with the radio. "All he had was a fracture in his leg and some cracked ribs."

"Wait a minute, hold er, Newt," I says. "Was this here guy on crutches? Big guy?"

"Yes –"

"Did he play defence for Yorkton by any chance?"

"I don't know!" she shrieks at me. I mean by this time her voice is so high and hysterical it was too much for me. I cannot stand to see women out of control like that, and I don't mean just women in wheelchairs neither. "I don't know!" she says. "My point is, what kind of god would let a man like Thorn die in a room with an animal like that? What kind of god . . ."

And you guessed it, she starts bawling right there in the dark. Jesus, I remember to this day. I can actually hear her if I put my mind to it. She bawls away and every time she comes up for air she sort of snorts? You know what I'm saying, like snorts so loud the whole elevator shakes? I didn't say nothing. I figured, hell, let her have her big moment up there. Chances are she don't have too much opportunity for a audience.

Just like yours truly, eh, Doc? What do you think? Not much of a audience out there, is there. When you got one, you make the most of it, eh?

"I keep thinking," you said, "if he had to die at sixty-four, could it not have been *me* in there with him? He could have had lovely music, intelligent conversation, he could have died in an atmosphere of sympathy, he could have had anything he wanted."

Ho boy. She was in for a real session that night. True confessions till the cows come home. She bawled away up there so long, Jesus, it was past three in the morning when she stopped. I checked my watch. Hell, I had time to light up half a dozen smokes. When she got to the nose-blowing stage, I up and asked her what you might say was a "key question."

"You ever heard tell of a guy named Archie Willens?"

She just about shit. "That's him!" she says. "You *know* him?"

"Know him? I played against him for four years."

"Well, if you ever play against him again, give him a nice maiming for me."

"He's not going to be playing in the senior league no more. Old Arch, he took a bad shot in that truck. I mean you been calling him down something fierce, you should of known that. He's got a pin in his leg now and he won't never skate normal. At best he can maybe play oldtimers'. And he didn't have no picnic in that hospital."

"You mean you're defending him? Did he tell you how he injured himself? He was bragging about it one day to the nurses. He got drunk and tried, in his *truck*, to chase an Indian man down a sideroad. There's your Archie Willens for you. The man he tried to run down ended up pulling him out of the wreck."

That was news to me. Mind you, I wouldn't put it past old Arch. When he pulls a real wild stunt like that he doesn't tell me no more. He knows I'll do a takeoff on him or tell him what a horse's ass he is. "He's like that," I says. "You gotta understand, he gets tanked up, he's a little wild. He don't mean nothing by it." I told her about how me and Arch got into a fight and how we got to be good friends afterwards. All's she wanted to know was did I paste him a good one. You can't talk to a woman like that. Too emotional.

Okay, I was wrong too, I admit it. There's things he never told me. And how much am I supposed to believe from a woman who's hysterical like you was, eh? How much am I supposed to believe? You better face up to it Doc, you was in bad shape.

Oops. Got carried away. She was in bad shape, this woman Anne. I keep forgetting who I'm talking to. Can you blame me, Doc? Can you see why I keep forgetting? I mean, if I play by the rule book and imagine this here third person, I get to feeling like some day I might end up on the funny farm with all them poets of yours.

*

Mr. Held, you are personalizing your monologues to such an extent that you forget your audience. I am not the person you'll be addressing for the rest of your life. Your audience, Mr. Held, is society. I am only here to work on your communication skills, and until you begin a more detailed reaction to the books on the course, I can scarcely begin this work, can I. In other words, Mr. Held, you are using your brief encounter in the elevator as an excuse to manufacture some relationship between us. You are using me as a crutch, Mr. Held.

*

I'm a fucking cripple! I'm a fucking cripple! I'm a fucking cripple! I'm a –

*

Not half as crippled as you think you are, Mr. Held. Now, will you attempt to respond to the reading material? I want your next tape by the end of the month.

*

Hey, Doc Wheels! How the fuck are ya? Oh, please beg your fucking pardon, I just called you by your name again. I sure am sorry, your highness. I hope this doesn't mean I've flunked your course. If you don't like it why don't you just take this here placater and –

Know what? These here tape machines aren't so hard to work after all. I just learned how to erase things. Maybe I'll just go back and erase the whole shooting match. You wouldn't like that much, would you, Doc? Maybe you would.

Maybe I should tell you what's pissing me off. Arch come in today. He has this limp, but it's looking twice as bad. Or maybe he's putting on the dog, eh? I was pretty honked off. I wanted to know if maybe he was the one got Charlotte knocked up in the first place.

"How's she goin?" he says.

"That depends," I says.

"On what?" he says.

"On whether you get off carryin your piss around in a briefcase."

"You're lucky," Arch says. "If you was a horse they woulda shot you."

I says, "Go ahead, Arch. Ready, aim, fire. No loss to the world. You could plank my woman till the cows come home."

He didn't say nothing. I guess I made my point. I guess I kind of pissed on his parade.

"Hey, Arch!" I says. "Don't get down in the dumps, old buddy. You got my girlfriend, I got your hospital bed, eh? Fair trade. Maybe some prof might come in here, share my room with me. Maybe if I'm nice to him, maybe he'll play my kinda music on the radio, eh? What do you think?"

"Who told you about me and Charlotte?" he says.

"Charlotte did. Who the fuck else?"

He swallows and his voice is real soft, like he's none too pleased with things. He mumbles something like, "That bitch." Made me wonder about whether Arch wasn't with Charlotte the night you and me had our all-nighter, Doc. Who knows how long them two was having their little party?

"Hey, Arch," I says, "you knocked off any smoked meat lately in the old half-ton? Huh?" Well, like I say, we had a real happy conversation.

What do you say? Did I give him that there maiming you was talking about? You didn't really want to hear me talk about no books, right?

Well, on with my story. I mean your story. I mean Doc Wheels' story. Meanwhile back at the old elevator, it's nothing to nothing and nobody's winning.

Must of been four o'clock in the morning. I'm laying down in a corner trying to get some shut-eye. She doesn't say much, old Doc Wheels. Just the same thing in this very low voice, over and over, "If only *I* could have been with him those last days, instead of *him*. If only it could have been *me*." Water under the bridge, as they say. Spilt milk.

Then maybe on towards four thirty, five o'clock, she says something else, this time louder. It woke me up. She says something about all that stuff in the hospital between

Arch and this Thorn dude was maybe part of a plan. Almost the only time she sounded like a Bible thumper to me. I don't remember much what she said. I was half asleep and she wasn't really talking to me, more like she was talking to herself. She said something about, maybe it was a test. Maybe that's His way of testing us. I says, What? And she says something about getting throwed in with your opposite. I was about to ask her to run that by me again when Jesus Christ if the lights didn't go on at that exact moment. A few seconds later I was out of that there elevator on the fourth, I run up to the fifth, I give her the candle and her kipper, and I'm free to go. Just like that.

That's when I seen her. Nothing like how I imagined. She was tall, pale and kind of skinny, but not bad at all. Nice face. I'd say more than halfway to being a considerable looker. Real blonde hair, not like Charlotte's. She wasn't no dye job.

We shake hands. Hers is very cold. I thank her and all, and take what you might call a "parting shot." I says to her, "Look," I says, "you been through a whole lot with that there prof dyin on you. I know what you're goin through. I mean I never knew the guy, eh, I just heard tell of him from Arch and you, but from what I can see, this here Thorn guy, he was what we call a grandstander in hockey. Like, he plays for the crowd? Well, I don't know what your job is all about, but on a team, we got no use for grandstanders. I mean them guys is so wrapped up in themselves they forget they're on a team, eh? And any bozo who gets up in front of a whole class of scholars and starts to piss and moan about 'it's time I up and kicked the bucket' or whatever, I say he's not worth one half of one third of sweet fuckall, scuse my French. That's the way I look at it," I says. "I'm sorry if I offended you and I appreciate what you done for me with your books and everything." I meant using her kipper but I said books because, well, anyways . . .

This is the part that keeps coming back the most frequent. I guess you know what I mean. I starts backing towards the stairway. You look up at me and say, "Come here. Just for a moment."

Hey, boys, not me. I'm heading out. I don't move. You start wheeling towards me. "You'll never know what it was like . . . for . . . me with him. You'll never know. Do you think I've never known desire, is that it?" You reach out your hand, and I guess it bothers me. It's like you was coming to get me. Because when I seen that bony hand coming at me, I just turn around and haul ass right out of there. I never looked back. I can only take true confessions so far. And I guess I draw the line at you talking sex to me like we was in the pool hall.

You're probably thinking I missed the point, eh, Doc? Here's this sonafabitch broken down hockey jock, never had no time for you, now he's flat on his back and making demands. You figure if you pay him one visit he'll say why not once a week, eh? I know, you got your life to live.

You know what I think? I think it's your turn to tell this here story. Good therapy, isn't that what you said? Why don't you give her a try? Remember, Doc, we got rules. None of this you-done-this you-done-that stuff. It's all he this and he that, right? His name's Gunnar and he wants to know what you're all about. Don't hold nothing back now, you hear?

Part 2
The Amorous
History of
Anne Walker

The Garden

When I was twelve, I was occasionally allowed to play in
the Montagues' yard. I'd be off like a shot, even though it
meant dressing up in a skirt and blouse. Their mansion
was one of two on the crescent. The other one, the Beausang mansion, was grander and to my eyes more exclusive.
A stile connected the two properties, and though my girl-
friends and I had climbed the Montagues' side of the stile
and gazed into the Beausang garden, we'd never crossed
over; that was forbidden. All we could see from the top of
the stile through the dense shrubbery were a few life-sized
statues, a fountain, a gazebo, and the outside of a huge
caragana maze. We spent hours fantasizing what would
happen to someone who got lost in the maze, and wondering what was at the centre. Perhaps only Carlyle, a large
dog chained somewhere on the grounds. Mrs. Montague

said he was a bog hound, whatever that is. We never saw him, but sometimes at night we heard him baying.

Once late in October my parents and I had supper at the Montagues'. When I was excused from supper, I was expected to join the Montague girls upstairs. But they were older than I and much too blasé about things I found enchanting, their own house, for instance, or the Beausang garden. So I left the youngest one, Ginia, to her records, and went outside to wander alone in their yard.

There was a full harvest moon. I climbed to the top of the stile. No longer was there any foliage to obscure my vision of the Beausang place. I couldn't see into the maze, of course, but for the first time in my life I could see the statues clearly, three of them. They were naked; their bodies had a bluish alabaster glow. The statue closest to me was a plump Cupid. He was crouching behind a bird bath, spying on the next closest statue: a lovely boy with a ribald grin, who in turn was peering from behind some bushes at the farthest statue: a girl leaping up from the centre of the fountain, leaping up and out of the water in a direction that would land her on the grass beside the bushes where the boy was crouched. Such stealth in the boy's bearing, such stealth in Cupid's, in my own. I looked up, suddenly suspicious that my mother or some adult was watching and would catch me in a shameful act. I scanned the Montagues' yard and house, from which Ginia's record was still blaring. I definitely felt watched. I scanned the Beausang's garden and something caught my eye, a dark figure next to the gazebo. He'd been there all along, eyeing me, and because he was dressed in a stable boy's dark uniform, and was black, I hadn't noticed him. We stared at each other for a long moment until I realized he too was a garden statue. He seemed to be pausing in his chores (carrying a saddle?) to watch me on the stile. And there I was, frozen into their pageant, part of their voyeuristic chain: the boy ogling the girl, the Cupid gloating at the boy, I swooning at the erotics of the situation as though through the very eyes of Cupid, and the stable boy giving me his own look of appraisal. It was all enchantingly wicked. I looked at the girl to see the direction of *her* glance. She was staring straight ahead at the entrance to the maze; she could see *into* the maze, and whatever she saw did not frighten her. She must have known what was at the centre. They all must have known. Was it Carlyle the bog hound, who would tear an interloper to pieces? Was it some sort of shrine? A wishing well, perhaps, that made people young forever? They were bewitched, and they knew something I didn't know.

Many times in my dreams I would cross that stile and try to play out the next scene on the lawn. Sometimes they would include me. The boy would leap after the girl, the Cupid would race after me, or me after the girl, or the girl after the stable boy, or the Cupid after the stable boy. . . . There were twenty permutations, if I kept the encounters one on one (but sometimes my mathematics turned profligate and the ratios rose). Just as often, however, they would all flee from me and remain out of reach, laughing and whispering around the next corner of the maze.

The song on Ginia's stereo that night was a vapid thing by a singer named Kay Starr; it was the one ingredient that never seemed to fit the pattern of magic. I was glad when Carlyle began at last to bay at the moon. It gave me something else to listen to. *C-c-hoom c-c-hoom cump cump cuhuh cuhuh cuhuh cump hm . . . hm . . . h-hm –*

The Stile

I have just turned fourteen and I've been allowed to attend the Montagues' garden party. Annual affair and very dressy. Robert Beausang appears to be the guest of honour. I've been eating cherries and strawberries soaked in rum from a cocktail glass. Robert Beausang has dredged them from the bottom of the punchbowl. We have strayed out past the ring of guests and meander beneath the poplars by the stile at the far end of the Montagues' yard. The peonies are in full bloom, snapdragons and huge delphiniums sway in and out of the shade. Crabapple trees just past their bloom shower petals all around us. It is just like confetti. There is a hot mad wind blowing and my dress and the other women's dresses toss and flare like the flowers.

Robert Beausang is more than twice my age, owns race horses, and talks to me as though I am much older, teasing me as he does all the women. According to Mother, who adores him, he has "quite a reputation." He's shaking his head at me. I've just told him I'm going to become an actress. Then maybe a writer. Both seem possible. Anything seems possible. "No," he says, "you'll go to Italy, fall in love with a count who races Ferraris, drinks heavily, and talks about death. You'll live in Cortina, have seven children, and pretend you're not from Edmonton. He will abandon you or die in the Monaco Grand Prix, and you'll become a femme fatale."

"How can you know what I'll be?"

"I can make a better stab at what you won't be. You won't be one of those neurotic bitches who wear sunglasses and call everyone dahling, and you won't go around writing things in cafés, looking sadder but wiser."

"You think you know everything about me," I reply, in what I consider to be a sophisticated tone, wondering: could it be true?

He sways a bit, spinning the stem of his glass between thumb and forefinger. "All right, forget the count. I'll tell you what you *might* be." He leans forward in a very intimate way and says, "You might just turn out to be very pretty . . . hm?"

Last night I dreamed of Robert Beausang. He says it like this. *You might just* (pausing as though to taste the first sip from a glass of wine, lips distended and moist) *turn out to be* (smiles like a hypnotist) *very pretty . . . hm?* (His voice hums this last little inflection, a note of insolence: we know you've seen yourself in the mirror, you little narcissist.)

It is one of my favourite memories. He was really looking at me; it was utterly personal. And a minute later, so was Mother, with great alarm. Not that I'd transgressed, but in a small blooming place in my mind, I'd dreamed of transgressing. One look and she knew. Those traces of fruit at the corners of my mouth? A blush, perhaps? Her worried look is an essential part of the memory; it validated the deliciousness of my moment by the stile.

There is a way your mother looks at you when you are fourteen, precocious, and on the way to being pretty. And a way men look at you. There is a way everyone looks at you. You don't understand the weight of their glances. You find it all a bit boring, sometimes pleasing. You get used to it, the expectation, the concern, the delight.

And then there is that other way people look at you as you rattle down the street in your wheelchair. In their eyes you are not becoming anything. You've already become it: stoic little saint, model invalid, a moral lesson on wheels for young people who think they've got it bad.

I had it bad. I found out in the fall of that same year.

The idea is to forget how people used to look at you and live with the way they see you now. One day it's Robert Beausang's fingers at my elbow guiding me lightly through the garden toward the Montagues' stile – leading me at last to that place the statues know about. The next day it's a motorized wheelchair that jolts me down the streets of another city.

Home is a small apartment in a big cement building equipped for people like me, wheelchair ramps, special railings and the like. So I'm grateful for that. But I've come to dread winters with their penetrating winds, and especially the ice that studs the sidewalks. When I rattle down an icy street, I sometimes feel every rut and bump right up through my spine. This is made worse by the occasional pressure sore on my backside. They look like halved apricots.

People who know tell me I'm one of the lucky ones. I have a job. I'm a sessional instructor on campus and I teach oral discourse by tape to quadraplegics. But this is romance, right? So romance you will get.

The Desk

For seven years I was a graduate student under Thornton Coldwell. For the first four I was Miss Walker. When he became my supervisor, I became Anne. The long talks began. First about my topic, then books in general, then life, then Thorn's life, and sometimes mine. An exchange of solitudes, the odd gift. I gave him a coffee mug with a sketch of Swift on the side; he gave me a candlestick and a slim white candle for my office. No doubt you will recall using that candle on a certain night when the power failed.

His office always seemed cold. It didn't matter what I wore, I ended up shivering. Whenever he showed concern I said it was my circulation. Partly true. One day he reached across his desk, and said, "Here," both hands extended. My gaze wandered from his hands, up the tweed sleeves of his jacket, to his florid face, his brilliant orange beard bristling out angrily, it seemed to me, at the profane world, his perpetually watery eyes, pale green like bay leaves. He wanted, he said, to warm my hands.

It became a habit. I realized he had needed to do this as badly as I had needed to have it done. And each time we conferred on my thesis, he would initiate the rite without a word by leaning forward, raising an index finger, and beckoning me to him. There we would sit like two people praying to each other instead of to God (and only He knows what Thorn was up to back then). His hands were large, pleasantly pudgy, bright pink like the skin on his neck, slightly moist, and always very warm. We'd speak as though nothing was happening, sometimes we'd even argue. I always wanted it to last and last, even after the leaning forward across his desk became very painful. I found ways of forgetting my pain while we sat there with our twenty fingers folded together in an orgy of snuggling. Pains gladly suffered at the altar of love. They would shoot up my back in time with my pulse and sometimes I almost groaned. He never knew.

"Do you think the world would frown on us?" he would ask; and "Yes," I would say, "I hope so."

His wife had been dead for several years when I met him, and if he had mistresses, no one ever told me. I doubt he did. In place of mistresses he had throngs of slobbering students who fluttered around him while he basked in their adoration. Oh, they fell for it, those mournful green eyes, the angry suffering face, the personal anecdotes, the witty assaults on rival scholars, the baritone voice that made the blinds and chairs vibrate in the room, that hint of an English accent, and all those old world histrionics behind the lectern. Such a gentleman, they would say. And in the fifth and sixth year, once a week, he was mine. All mine.

Until one day late in the winter. I was wearing a thin sweater. And it was colder than it should have been, and I regretted having taken off my coat in his office. I shivered through the preliminaries of my thesis proposal, shivered through the account of how much he loathed every minute of the faculty council budget debate, shivered during our handholding devotions, until finally he asked, "Are you well? Can I get you something?" And the child inside – no, by God, the woman – said, "I need you to warm me."

I saw something gathering in around his eyes, perhaps a struggle between professional reticence and that thing in men that makes them skulk around vulnerable-looking girls. Did I see a trace of Robert Beausang right then? I think so. I think I was finally crossing the stile. It began with a businesslike chafing of arms. It ended rather differently. He carried me to his chair. I found myself looking from his lap across the imposing expanse of his mahogany desk, the one that until now had always been between us, peering from his point of view at my empty wheelchair, imagining myself still *in* the wheelchair (as his hand found its way beneath my sweater and began its upward journey), imagining myself leaning forward to watch this shameless spectacle with a shocked look until – it was sudden – he was kissing me, he had barely caressed – well, you can imagine what he caressed, it was like a button going UP and I began to rock uncontrollably, my body hiccoughed in the throes of some erotic epilepsy, I was glowing with warmth, rocking with hot spasms.

Which frightened him. And he stopped, plainly stricken by my body's untimely revolution. He didn't even ask if I'd enjoyed it. Such pleasure was clearly beyond his wildest imaginings. I knew, then, that he would say it well before he did, exactly the wrong words: "I'm sorry, Anne."

I expected a gradual cooling on his part, nothing sudden. Imagine my surprise when, on the following Monday, I received a memo from the graduate chairman saying something to the effect that owing to Professor Coldwell's upcoming sabbatical, I would be assigned a new thesis supervisor. The sort of arrangement two mature men would make after discussing, coolly and earnestly, Miss Walker's tragic yearnings; they would call it a compassionate decision, best for all parties. Give her a chance to come to her senses.

Thin-blooded bastard. I never told him to his face, of course, but it was true. He was a thin-blooded tepid egotistical bastard. Are you listening? This is one thing I cannot stand in a man. And I'm not reading this, I'm saying it, so in case you've got some idea of me as a shrinking violet draped over a wheelchair, forget it, all right? You want plain speaking? You'll get plain speaking. Is that plain enough for you? *Ku-huck, ku-huck ku-huck-huck-huck* –

Anyway . . . when Thorn came back from his sabbatical – Am I embarrassing you? Honestly, I hope I'm not embarrassing you. When Thorn came back, we engaged in a lukewarm friendship, but of course it wasn't the same. He'd returned early because of his cancer. He insisted on working, teaching, right up to the last possible day. I kept wanting to comfort him but he would have none of it. We exchanged civilities right up to the end. Not once, though, did we speak of our little assignations in room 544.2.

Whatever one calls it, an affair of the heart, a crush, passing ships, I'm glad of it. I allowed it, it tasted good, bitter, all those things love is supposed to taste like. I suppose it shows. A way of smiling, perhaps, when someone makes an off-colour joke? A look of tolerance, even of fondness, at the young lovers who stroll through the campus, the demonstrative ones? A certain tumescence of style in my spring lectures? I remember thinking last month that I really ought to wheel over to the cemetery with a wreath of flowers and thank Thorn.

But I couldn't. I'd stopped murdering him but I was still burying him, and with him, all my servile gratitude.

The Elevator

As you are probably aware, this is where you came in. Brash, big on beer drinking, hockey playing, bowling women over, short on patience. And not big on modern poetry, and definitely not fond of stuck elevators. I must admit, I'm not used to men like you.

In defence of the books I fed you through the crack in the elevator doors, I must remind you that there was no space for thicker books. It was modern poetry collections or nothing. English departments do not, as a rule, stock their shelves with copies of *Sports Illustrated*, girly magazines, or action novels. And if the poetry of Sylvia Plath, or her ilk, was not your cup of tea, what was *I* to do about it? You filled my leg bag with your urine, burned my candle to the stub, ripped two of my dust jackets, and I'm supposed to feel apologetic for the books I gave you?

I will admit, the night we spent in the Arts Building was . . . extraordinary. And yes, we did settle into some nice talk. And I'll also admit it was troubled times for me. I needed someone to talk to. But as far as you were concerned, that was it. Once you were out of that elevator, you plopped my leg bag in my lap, gave me one of your smarmy grins, and raced out the door. Not one phonecall to thank me, no note, no visits. You'd made up your mind about me, Gunnar: submissive invalid with heart of gold, self-sacrificing to a fault. Weird taste in reading. End of story.

And now you've joined the ranks of the gimps (again, your term). You don't sleep well, you won't take medication, you refuse food, you heap abuse on the nurses, and revile all the women who visit you.

And you want *me* to visit you? Presumably it is *my* turn to be abused, is that it? I've listened to your tapes, this last one twice. You wanted to know, so now you know, it's all here: the amorous history of Anne Walker in a – *cump cuhuh cuhuh cuhuh c-c-cum c-cum hm hum . . . hm –*

I'll admit one more thing: yes, I've thought about you, about our long night with the elevator door between us. But you will understand me, won't you, Gunnar, if I tell you it was not one of my favourite meetings?

What if those doctors are right? What if you have your operation and become ambulatory (for people who don't read, that means walkers)? And what if I start to visit you, say once a week, as you suggest? Does this mean when you get healthy again you'll just skate back to your little –

There I go, flying off the handle. The more angry I get, the more I cough, and up goes the needle on my volume register. I don't like tape recorders. I'd much rather write things down.

I'm scribbling away at a poem. The only time I get to work on poems is when I'm sick. This one's about love and elevators. In love, as in elevators, certain doors are closed so that certain heights and depths can be reached. There's always the fear of falling. Malfunctions can occur. And if they do, one becomes dependent upon someone *outside*, do you see? And how do you trust that person? Well, it's simple; you have to. You've lost all your choices. . . .

I'm avoiding something, I know.

It's the coughing. When I cough it feels as though a part of me leaves. Sometimes I feel as though . . . wherever my coughs are flying to . . . Thorn is waiting there, to finish something. I may see him again, do you see, it's just a matter of letting go. Sometimes I think Thorn is coughing me.

Sometimes, like this morning, I think my lungs may decide to get a bit better, and then it's just me coughing again.

Oh, I had a dream last night. You and I met on an elevator, one that worked. You were in uniform, skates and all, holding a hockey stick. The elevator went up past my office on the fifth floor without even slowing down, past History, Philosophy, and Religion on the tenth; it rose up and up above the city. I could see a great expanse of parkland and prairie below, and still it ascended, into a vast white fold of clouds. It finally stopped at a turnstile. We went through, you on skates pushing me in my wheelchair. We stopped before the Beausang maze. The statues were huddled together whispering, and when they saw me there, with you, they were astounded. Something about them was different though. They'd grown into young adults.

The black one looked more like a tennis pro than a stable boy. "There must be some mistake," he said to both of us.

"Nope," you said, holding up a card. "Says here, 'Anne Walker.' "

The statues ran on into the maze, so we followed. It

turned out to be an inner garden, with huge flowers everywhere. I think they were mostly snapdragons. They had
long lolling tongues and were so big they leaned over us
like huge friendly dogs. We all sat in lawn chairs and
listened while a man read a lecture. He was very serious. It
had something to do with the tending of flowers.

Meanwhile the flowers began to lick us. This irritated
you, and you began pushing them away. The man lecturing to us, I realized suddenly, was Thorn. He wore a splen-
did tweed jacket and wool plaid tie, but he'd forgotten to
put his trousers on. His shorts were striped, almost knee-
length, and he wore long dark socks with garters. I started
to laugh but the girl statue, who was taking notes, turned
around to hush me. I just couldn't stop laughing. People
kept giving me looks. Finally I had to wheel myself out of
there. You came too. It was hot in the maze. Music was
playing. The flowers nodded above us, nuzzling each other
and licking promiscuously in every direction. We came
into a clearing, it was near the gazebo. You started to tear
off your skates and clothes until you were down to your
hockey pants and helmet. I was listening to the music. I
don't think I was wearing anything. The music had words
to it, it was Ginia Montague's record from back in the
fifties. It went

> *One two and then rock,*
> *One two and then roll,*
> *One two and then jump,*
> *It's good for your soul,*
> *It's old but it's new,*
> *Let's do the rock and roll waltz.*

"Wanna dance?" you said.

"Don't be silly," I said, but you held out your hand, and,
"Yes," I said. "Why not?"

The dance went like this. Instead of facing each other we
stood side by side, holding hands. We'd take two steps
forward and then jump as far as we could. Then two more

steps and a big jump. We went through the whole garden that way. It was all right, I suppose. I had a good time.

"So, big deal," I hear you say. "It's only a dream." And maybe my lungs' improving, maybe that's only a dream too. And maybe that operation of yours they keep talking about, maybe that's only a dream. I mean, I do plan to visit you. Not all night long, as you first suggested, but a nice little visit. So just in case it isn't a dream, and one day you look up and I'm sitting there in your room, I think I'd better warn you, Gunnar, I'm not that great a dancer.

This World

Whenever Jimmy Goggins walked home at night in the cold weather, his cheeks went as red as ripe nectarines. He had a pronounced turnout, so as he crunched along the snowy walks, his rotund body would rock from side to side. His students called him Jolly Jimmy. This was partly because his grade XI physics class was known as Jolly Rockets, but mainly because he laughed a lot, even when people were teasing him. On this particular night, however, as he carried home his package of pastry (still warm inside the bag), something about him was different. He was a bit stooped, his eyes unfocussed, his lips contracted, as though nothing around him could be as important as the thoughts he was having.

Connie. He could remember some of her words, but no longer the sound of her voice – only the fact that he had liked it. He could remember the pay phone (lobby of the Sutherland Beer Parlour), the day (New Year's Eve), the amount he had drunk (three Bo Maids, six or seven draft, and a whisky someone had bought him). He could also remember the song he had played on the touchtone buttons. It was "Mary Had a Little Lamb." But try as he would, every time he dialled this tune on his own phone, he got Schmeizer's Hot Tubs, and no (said the woman with the monotone voice), no one named Connie worked there. Perhaps, when he was playing his tune on New Year's, he'd jazzed up the original. He had never actually been drunk before. But perhaps if he got *just* as drunk (three Bo Maids, six or seven draft, and a whisky), he would remember exactly how he had played it. Connie seemed to like him, she laughed at one of his remarks (he forgot which one), but she declined to give him either her last name or her number. He could hardly blame her.

Beneath the lock on his mailbox the name of the previous tenant, Bottoms, was printed on a green plastic label. Today, only junk mail.

He began the slow spiral up to his garret. Bottoms indeed. The name seemed to follow him around these days. From his apartment door, to his mailbox, the character (minus an s) in this year's school play, back home to the mailbox and the apartment door. It made him think of his predecessor in this apartment as a bizarre young man with the head of an ass, in love with a fairy queen. Goggins ripped the green plastic label off his door. Farewell Bottom the Weaver, hail Jimmy Goggins, Seeker of . . .

Connie.

He faltered in this little revery. He had not wanted to come home to an empty apartment, but had no reason not to. As the winter progressed, this situation arose quite often. The day was almost gone, people were going home, and he could not summon much appetite for his own company. He would rather have cooked for two than one. He found watching television comedies and cop shows demoralizing. Most of his friends were married or in Winnipeg. The married ones always seemed busy when he phoned them. So he had to set up a program of rewards for going home, a mental list:

THINGS TO LOOK FORWARD TO FROM SUPPERTIME TILL
MIDNIGHT, MONDAY, JANUARY 13

1) Make supper a festive affair
2) Gooey delights from Turner's Bakery
3) Cup of tea to go with gooey delights
4) Put on Divine Mozart or equiv. to go with #3 above
5) Phone female – any female – ask self over for coffee. *Do* it this time
6) Alternate plan if #5 above fails; more Div. Mozart or equiv. followed by
7) Hot bath
8) Hot chocolate
9) Chapter or two of Asimov
10) Exotic fantasy – very lurid – just before beddybyes
11) 10 Hail Marys
12) Count blessings, money, sheep
13) . . .

Unlucky number. Lately, like Bottom's name, it had been showing up all over the place. The last two digits of the school phone number, the chapter he was teaching from *Modern Physics, Book One*, everywhere. And just as he threw his coat on the bed, he remembered it was the thirteenth of January. His thirteenth item on the list would be for Connie to phone. She hadn't yet, though once the phone *had* been ringing when he came in from Thursday-night shopping. Three or four seconds more and he would have had it. You never knew. He looked out his kitchen window at the snow banked up beside the road, a chill blue beneath the fluorescent streetlight. Private pleasures, Goggins. A bath, yes. A big beautiful soporific soaking. He thought fondly of the huge old enamel tub in the bathroom. It would be steaming with hot water. Say what she might about the ad hoc state of his apartment, Connie would adore his old bathtub.

Goggins snapped on his little bedside wakeup radio in time to hear a man, from New York obviously, extolling Vivaldi in the most extravagant terms.

"Supper," he announced to the apartment, rubbing his hands together. A squalid affair for most bachelors, but Goggins knew one end of a skillet from the other. He knew too that there was still one halibut steak in the old fridge.

RECIPE FOR HALIBUT STEAK GAUGUIN

1 large halibut steak at least 1″ thick
1 tbsp chopped parsley
1 glob of butter
1 handful of sliced mushrooms
1 mega-glob of sour cream
1 cup or so of dry white wine
pinch salt
pinch pepper
dash cumin
1 hour Vivaldi

Arrange steak in shallow greased baking dish, season with salt and pepper. Bake at 450⁰ F for ten minutes. Turn up Vivaldi full blast. Melt butter, sauté mushrooms until golden. Sample white wine before and after measuring. Remove mushrooms from heat and stir in sour cream, wine, more salt and pepper. Pour sauce over fish and sprinkle with cumin. Forget anxiety over having to pick team of cheerleaders from army of nymphets, forget derisive laughter of over-sexed colleagues, forget time wasted on set for school play, forget everything including name, address, phone number, social insurance number, chequing account, etc. Reduce heat to 375⁰ F and bake five minutes. Sample resampled wine. Resample resampled wine. Open oven and do not sniff but smell waftings from Pacific, let aroma humanize and thaw you. Bless halibut, let it receive salivation. Garnish with parsley. Serves Goggins.

Vegetables were a problem. His broccoli had gone limp and at various points of contact with its plastic bag had gone black. Delicately Goggins disposed of the broccoli. There were still some peas in the freezer. Frozen in. His freezer looked like the inside of a hastily abandoned igloo. He found a screwdriver, chipped and spiked his way into the frozen peas. *Petis pois*, the package said. *Qualité de gourmet*. He did them in his steamer. Add yogurt and serve.

Ravenous, almost happy, Goggins sat down to supper. The man from New York said that Vivaldi's something-or-other in D was not an o.t.w., not a super-o.t.w., but a super-super-o.t.w. composition. Goggins would not have put it quite that way, but he agreed. Bon appetit, he said to the man from New York, who explained that o.t.w. was out of this world.

The bathtub is ready. Goggins gloats big, white, and naked over its surface for a moment, then steps in gingerly. The ranging emptiness of his garret begins to lose its insistence. One leg in, to the knee. Ouch. Two legs to the knee. Down, Goggins. No, Goggins. Down, I said, down. Ow! E-e-e-ase in the haunches. Haunches lowering, genitals recoiling, then ouch! Yike! Ow! Ooh! Ahh. Yes, ahh. Lovely, ahhhhhh.

Goggins feels consummated. Apple-cheeked and drained of energy, he muses on the displacement of bodies in bathwater. His penis bobs, boiled and languorous on the surface. He looks beyond to his toes at the far end of the tub, a chain of pink islets. The water has become too soapy to find the soap. He feels steamed, generously, down and in, laved, soothed, his tight centres growing languid. He is awake in his own huge dream of wallowing. He thinks about physics. Physics. He thinks about world strife. World Strife. He thinks about the immortality of the human soul. Immortality of Human Soul. He thinks about the universals, all the universals, there they all are. He thinks about . . .

Love. He is the Great Porpoise Man. He bathes with the whales and oogles the sirens fat and bulbous clustering on the rocks, combing out their long hair. Boobies bobulating. Walrus Woman. His eyes meet hers, compelling her to swim out for him. Then one by one they all leave their rocks for the steaming water. Swimming out toward the pink buoy, taking their time, undulating their swollen bodies for him, he circling slowly. The snow falling and melting on his shoulders, he submerging among the undulant bodies, surfacing to breathe in the hot sulphur air. She cruising closer, mesmerized by the bigness of his body, the power of his regular stroke. As her body passes he feels the hot softness of her flesh, she silent, fluttering her tail fin and then slowly, not too –

"Brrrrrrringgggggg!"

"It never goddam fails!"

Like a sounding whale Goggins surged from his bath. The wake from his body ran the length of the tub and splashed over the bathtub rim onto the floor. He dripped over to his robe vowing never again to leave the phone on its cradle while he was in the tub. It had begun its fourth ring when Goggins reached it, his blue towelled bathrobe approximately around him. Enervated, dripping, he snatched up the receiver.

A somewhat hoarse feminine voice said, "I would like to speak to a Mr. Jim Goggins. Please." She spoke slowly and methodically, lugging each word into place. "You might not remember me," she added.

"I'm afraid I don't follow you," said Jimmy. He was having problems with his robe.

"Mary had a little lamb, little lamb, little lamb . . . Mary had a little lamb, her fleece was white as snow."

"You're Connie?"

"Right!" said the voice, drawing out the word so that it slid a good octave down the scale.

"I didn't recognize your voice."

"Well, on New Year's Eve I wasn't drinking, was I? You were the one hitting the bottle, hey? Now it's my turn. Here's to you, Jimmy Goggins." He heard a clunk against her receiver. "Here's to me, Connie Smith. How ya doin?" She hiccoughed. "Tell me, Jimmy – can I call you Jimmy? – tell me, what do you think about girls who drink – I mean just once in a while. You know, just tie one on for the hell of it, hey?"

"You sound different," he said, and realized he'd already mentioned something to that effect.

"Well, so do you, Bub. I mean when you phoned me I was cold sober. Give a girl a break, hey?"

"Sorry," he said.

"You're sorry!" she cried. "Sorry! Jesus . . ." He heard something hard and heavy, perhaps a radio, crash to the floor. After a while she said, "I forgot what I was saying. What was I saying?"

"Something about drinking."

"You know something, Jimmy? Can I call you Jimmy? You know something? I like you. You're probably a pretty decent guy, hey? You know something? The night you phoned? You know what I was doing New Year's Eve on the night you phoned? Me, a knockout, I mean I'm a real knockout, I'll admit it, why should I hide it, an army of guys tells you you're a knockout, you must be a knockout, right? Well, when you phoned, I was sitting here alone in my apartment just wondering . . ." Suddenly she stopped. There was a long silence and the sound of a chair scraping. He thought he heard panting and sniffling. After a long pause she sang out, "Allo-allo-allo, just had to let the cat out. Where was I?"

"You were telling me about what you were doing on New Year's."

"I was? So I was. Anyway, thanks."

"Thanks for what?"

"Well, Jesus, Jimmy, haven't you been listening? No one ever listens to you. No one ever really listens. You know that? Hey, enough about me. Tell me about yourself."

"I'm a bachelor," he said, and couldn't think of anything else to say.

"I'll bet you really mow em down, right? I bet you've got a girl in every port. Hey, let me ask you," she whispered, and started to snicker. "Let me ask you, Jimmy, when you're . . . you know, gettin it on, do you talk? No guff, now. Do you *talk*?"

"Well, it depends," he said, and wondered if it wouldn't be better just to hang up.

"I like it when they talk to me. . . ." There was a long pause and another hiccough.

"Connie?"

Again he heard the sound of a scraping chair and then the clink of glass on glass. He wanted to tell her that he was having a bath, and wouldn't she rather call him when she was sober. He looked over at the wet bathroom floor, the footprints on his carpet, down at one of his boiled red legs. He could feel the wind sifting through a crack in the old storm window behind him. It felt very cold on his neck.

"Connie?"

"Allo-allo, it's me again. Hope you didn't die of old age. Had to let out the cat. Anyway, that's why I phoned you, Jimmy."

"Why?"

"Do you ever listen to anything a girl says? I *told* you. I just phoned to thank you for phoning me. I mean . . . it was that bad, you know? I was a basket case. You should've seen me. Shaking like a leaf. This girl I work with she says it's nerves, I should take yeast. A fat lot she knows, hey? A fat lot she knows. Hey, Jimmy, you ever been to the top of Lacombe Tower? You know, the can of Raid, as folks around here say. You ever been up there?"

"No."

"That's where I work now. At the restaurant. Right on top. Goes around an round. Around an round an round she goes. Where she stops nobody knows. Herman the German he's our boss. Makes us wear these full-length black jobbies. Very slinky, hey? You ever see us serving up drinks?"

"I've never been there," he said again.

"Well, you're not missing much. I've been there maybe a month. You suck up to the big spenders you get fifty bucks a night. Big deal. I'm only there for a while. Make a few bucks and move on. I'm not your typical waitress. I'm actually a musician. Bet you didn't know that, hey, Jimmy?"

Goggins perked up at this last bit of news. "What do you play?"

"I'm a flute player. I had a try-out with the symphony. Guy who auditioned us, he was the assistant conductor, he said I reminded him of Catherine Deneuve. Have you ever heard a bigger load of horseshit in your entire life? And do you know what? I *fell* for it."

"Can you play that dance from *The Nutcracker*?" He tried to think of the name. It was very popular around Christmas time. It was right on the tip of his tongue.

"You name it, Bub, I can play it."

What would she wear when she played her flute? Something diaphanous, he fancied. But also very proper. Could you have both? he wondered.

"This guy, his name was Edvard. He spelled it E-d-v-a-r-d. I mean, he wouldn't be caught dead spelling his name like an ordinary mortal, not him. All the girls must have been ga-ga over him. All you ever heard at the auditions was Edvard this and Edvard that. I mean this guy was so vain he probably stood in front of the mirror each morning and practised brooding for an hour before rehearsals. I caught him one morning."

"You caught him?"

"Yeah, he was trimming his moustache. I swear he was in love with his own face. I mean, the way he was *looking* at his reflection. That's when he told me I'd lost out to this *lady*. He calls her a lady. Some lady. You can guess how *she* won all her auditions, hey? He says to me, he says, 'We really loved your playing, Connie. It's not that we didn't love your playing. It came down to a question of repertoire and Vanessa' – this chick's name was Vanessa – 'and Vanessa had the repertoire.' You ask me, she had the wardrobe. I asked him what about all that malarkey about me reminding him of Catherine Deneuve and do you know what he said? I mean we'd scarcely been out of the sack for an entire week and he said, 'Connie, Catherine Deneuve is an actress, not a flautist.' " She hiccoughed.

Goggins muttered something about what an irresponsible fellow this Edvard seemed, but apparently Connie didn't hear him. She had abandoned the telephone once again. He listened for the sound of her chair or her glass but heard nothing. It was plain to him that she needed someone. A good man. She needed a steady understanding chap who would talk some sense into her. She'd get over this Edvard character soon enough. His type was a dime a dozen.

Jimmy was getting chilly, but he was no longer tempted to hang up. He began to wonder again what Connie looked like. She would have a tragic look, he decided. She would play plaintive things on her flute and her eyes would wander from the sheet music to some faraway place where love was a joyful uncomplicated feeling. Her bed would have a lacey coverlet. It was then that he resolved to ask her out on a date.

He could hear her blowing her nose. After a moment she returned to the line.

"Some conversation, hey? First you and then me. Did

some chick give you the slip? No? I bet you're married. Hey, Jimmy? Come on now, you can tell me. I won't squeal."

"I told you. I'm a bachelor."

"Edvard was married. He said he didn't want our relationship as he called it to exist in this world. It was a fantasy, he said. I mean, do you believe this turkey? He got a conducting job in Hamilton. I hope he chokes on the smog."

"He sounds unworthy of you."

"He sounds unworthy of you," she said in a nasal voice. "Where in the world did you dig that one up? Hey, I take it back, Jimmy. We're still friends, right? Even if you are a goddam rake. Hey, what do you say we go out and have a drink some time? Do you think you'd like that?"

"Sure," Jimmy said, and felt a faint rush of blood.

"You mean you'd have a drink with an old reject like me? Jesus Murphy, no accounting for taste. It's not like I'm hustling you, it's not like that, you understand, Jimmy. You mean it? You'd really go out for a drink some time?"

The water had gone lukewarm. He turned on the hot and let it run for a while, then turned it off. He could hear the January wind. It was rattling the old frames of his storm windows. And blowing at Connie's window too? Around and round and round she goes. Where she stops, nobody knows. . . . Did she get cold at night?

He had a date with her, a date with a girl who looked like Catherine Deneuve. She sat and played birdlike melodies on the flute and served people in a full-length black jobby.

He looked down thoughtfully at his bobbing penis and beyond to his toes. They were neither buoys nor islets, they were a penis and ten toes. And the water had cooled again. He lifted the plug. Only with a great effort could he imagine what went on down there beneath the soapy emulsion:

the Great Porpoise Man swimming eagerly after the sirens
and Walrus Woman as they all spiralled madly down the
drain. Where was Bottom the Weaver? It didn't matter. He
half felt the urge to wave goodbye to them, to tell them he
was going out on a date with a girl who looked like Catherine Deneuve; tell them why he was now so happy, and
why so sad.

Getting
the Word

1

Casey has recently learned the knack of walking with
Anton Kvintz; she manages about three strides to every two
of his. She is scarcely an inch over five feet and he is well
over six. In their many walks together she has done all the
compromising, pumping her short muscular legs so fast
that her bum-length brown hair shakes wildly all down
her back. She never tells him to slow down; she has learned
to let his compulsions run their course. Besides, she likes
to walk with Kvintz.

He is long-limbed and uncommonly bony. Some would
say cadaverous. Young aspiring writers, girls in search of
tortured genius, in fact many people of a romantic persua-
sion, are drawn to that gaunt frame, the suffering mouth,
the ancient blue raincoat he claims to have borrowed several years ago from Leonard Cohen, the lobo shadow he
casts, perenially haunting the campus like his own ghost.

His eyes are Bliss Carman sad, or so his landlady told him
not long ago.

Anyone watching him climb the old dark stairway of
Assiniboia Hall might, however, note just a trace of spring
to his step, perhaps just the faintest suspicion of hope in
his eyes, which are peering at the door of the gloomy third-
floor landing, the last barrier to a new revelation. Kvintz
would capitalize the word revelation at this point. He met
her only a week ago in Assiniboia Hall, in the coffee
lounge. She is older than Casey, more mature in every way,
tall (Casey is stacked and stubby), lynx-eyed, her hair a
great round garland of brown curls. She is very bright, by
all accounts. Fresh out from Montreal. She seems to take in
everything with her eyes, wears no wedding ring. Her
poems, collected in *Canuckle Sandwich*, have become na-
tionalist feminist rallying cries. She introduced herself as
the new creative writing instructor. Overwhelmed after a
brief conversation, he forgot her name. He handed her a
manila envelope, burbled an apology, and fled into the
November dusk.

In a moment he gets the word from her. On his writing,
that is. If she likes it, then there is hope for something . . .
something he's been fantasizing all week. A denial of the
greyness of Edmonton in November. To describe the fantasy would be to demean it.

Plants. Trees. Animals. She seemed to know a lot about
them. Today Kvintz wears his mackinaw, faded jeans,
climbing boots. His hair blows free, unleashed from its
elastic band. The effect is woodsy: without having to ask
him, she would assume he knew one end of a canoe from
the other.

At this moment she sits in her office with his manuscript
on her desk. Perhaps she is shivering; the weather has
turned cold as death. She is probably lonely.

Kvintz would not write it this way. He is anxiously alive
in the midst of this narrative, so anxious that he has quite
lost his perspective.

We shall not lose ours. This is the third year Kvintz has been making these trips to Assiniboia Hall, a crumbly castellated residence which has been converted into an English department. Kvintz is a graduate student, a recidivist, as he calls himself. He has discovered that the only way to continue his subsidized existence writing his works-in-progress is to renew his graduate student status each fall. Sometimes they make him take a seminar to demonstrate his fidelity to the system, or compile lists of library holdings. He submits to these indignities each time with a mournful look, knowing that to do otherwise would involve an end to his life of tortured but free meditation in his garret. The sixties are almost over, he is nearly thirty, his ponytail turning grey. Recently he has been unable to imagine any other way of life.

The corridor is badly lit. He knocks lightly on her door. It swings slowly from the timid force of his knuckles, the crack widens before him and a slash of brilliant sunlight from her office window lights up the gloomy hallway. Kvintz squints.

This door will take its time opening, the reader should be warned. There is much to learn in the meantime. For one thing, Casey Jones is waiting for Kvintz in the downstairs foyer of Assiniboia Hall. For another, she is very unhappy about this. Kvintz is not aware of this second fact, but he will be.

2

In the beginning, there was Bitney. He was Kvintz's first creative writing supervisor, a tall pale Liverpudlian in his mid-thirties, of slight build and uncertain temperament. He was the first professor to read Kvintz's works-in-progress. His hair was modishly long, but stringy, and shorter than Kvintz's ponytail. He always wore jeans and scuffed Beatleboots with pointed toes, and at work often wore a purple velvet jacket of an Edwardian cut over his T-shirt. He was a kind of last sad echo of Carnaby Street as the world moved inexorably toward the seventies. Yet in some ways, which Kvintz came to find disconcerting, he was a very old-fashioned man, a voice from the Empire gone out to the colonies to make a bit of lolly.

During office hours, shortly after settling in Canada, he took to sitting amid the clutter and mold of his office in a state of perpetual culture shock. Cartons of musty unpacked boxes surrounded a desk stacked with unmarked essays and unfinished manuscripts. The mold was real. He was a half-finisher of burgers, fish and chips, fruit and pizza. Kvintz observed that whereas a man with half as many university degrees would throw these unfinished delicacies into the waste-basket, Bitney would toss them into the drawers of his desk, his filing cabinet, or stack them on his bookshelves.

Kvintz marvelled over Bitney's lust for junk food. He had always expected better of an Englishman. For example, Bitney had never heard of Murchie's tea. He didn't even drink tea, only machine coffee for his daily hangovers. He loved potato chips (which he called crisps) most of all. Empty crumpled bags of Old Dutch lay in his wake wherever he wandered. When the history of Bitney's doleful career in Edmonton was told, it would be based on very few written documents but many crumpled bags of Old Dutch, most of which lay in the gutters between his apartment and the Strathcona Hotel beer parlour, in a three to one ratio to the bags that clustered around the gutters between his apartment and his Assiniboia office.

"For a brief period," Kvintz recounts, "I wanted to tell him how to take care of himself over here. Stop stashing bottles of whisky in his desk, learn to do some cooking and a little cleaning up. I wanted to teach him to be an Englishman. But every time he opened his mouth, even then I knew . . ." *Bloozzy hell, y'iv nivver read him. He's real gear, y'know.* Real gear. Real fab. Perhaps Bitney thought he had to talk like that to his students. Like most of the other baby-boom hirings he came to Edmonton when the Beatles were at the height of their popularity. Perhaps speaking Liverpudlian was Bitney's last contact with his origins and his only method of seeming more with it than he was.

Scarcely anything Kvintz wrote ever pleased Bitney. Bitney would write extensive comments down the margins of Kvintz's stories and poems. They were penned in neat precise vicious prose which seemed to contradict the campy garble that escaped Bitney's mouth. Bitney was so slack about marking other students' assignments that, from the outset, there were complaints about him. But he was never late with Kvintz's work. He seemed, in fact, to love this weekly act of derision. Perhaps it was some obscure form of cultural affirmation. Kvintz's long poem on the beluga was "plainly circumscribed by its subject matter." Of course, Kvintz hastened to tell Casey, Bitney missed the point entirely. But when he tried to explain to Bitney the politics of Hudson's Bay whaling, Bitney shook his head from side to side: *No-no, no-no, no-no, no, no, no.* Kvintz's meditation on Crowfoot was a "florid excretion." His satire on the NHL "dies of terminal cuteness on page one, paragraph one." Finally he handed Kvintz a dusty stack of English writers with orders to read every one of them before Christmas.

And something must have happened from that experience, a sea change in Kvintz's imagination. Because he began writing in a new vein. No more animal poems, no more satires. Just sketches, Kvintz would call them. He handed several to Bitney, waited for one week, then made the sweaty journey to Assiniboia Hall to get the word from Bitney. He did not hate him, mind you, but if that day Bitney took one more cheap shot at his writing, he would disembowel the man with his own letter opener.

As the door of his still nameless supervisor's office swings into a wash of sunlight, he is caught in the swirl of a *déjà vu*. The feeling now is different, however, and he knows it. Because he remembers how it felt with Bitney that time.

"Her-herm," he had said.

Bitney looked up from the soccer scores in *The Manchester Guardian*, removed the sunglasses which he habitually wore until dark. This he did while avoiding eye contact with Kvintz. Kvintz knew then that his latest offerings were execrably bad, according to the bloodshot eyes of his mentor. Bitney really was a roaring asshole; that's all there was to it.

"Well, Mr. Kvintz," said Bitney. He noticed that Bitney had an ugly scrape on the chin, partially covered by a bandage. He absolutely refused at that moment to ask Bitney about his sketches. He asked him, therefore, about the scrape on his chin.

"I were leggin after a moggy," Bitney replied. Kvintz had learned that, indeed, moggies were cats. He assumed, therefore, that Bitney had, in his cups, been chasing a cat.

"After a few bevvies, like, in the S'rathcona," added Bitney.

Kvintz realized that this man was simply softening him up for the old one-two punch. Beware of pleasantries. He looked down at the faded feathered cuffs of his own jeans, then up at Bitney's desk. Beneath a brown apple core were his new sketches.

"Yes," said Bitney. "I read yer masterwerk there, like."

"My masterwork?" enquired Kvintz.

"Yer Edmonton sketches. 'The New Romanians.' I liked it, sort of."

Bitney has just said he liked the work. I liked it, that's what he said.

"Bag o' crisps?" offered Bitney, indicating some potato chips spilled from a bag on the corner of his desk. Kvintz picked up a potato chip, and though it smelled of something, like old bologna, he put it in his mouth. Perhaps Bitney was not such a bad guy after all. "I trust we'll be seein more of this novel. It could be real fab stoof."

Yes, nodded Kvintz. Of course. Already he was forming plans. He could force these sketches into a single, compelling narrative. A veritable epic about Romanian immigrants beginning with his great grandfather, the last of the Kvintz line to have lived in Romania, Anton Kvintz the first. He was only a yellowed photograph to Kvintz but Kvintz had no trouble at all visualizing the man as a boy herding sheep at the foot of the Transylvanian Alps. The novel he planned would treat each generation down to his own, ending with a young man in Edmonton who hungered for knowledge of his roots, hungered for love, peace, brotherhood. . . . Now it came to him in a flash: this young man would become his model for alienated, suffering humanity. He would amble lonely and troubled through the streets of Edmonton. This was only the beginning. It was worth an o.f.y. grant in the summer and a Canada Council next winter. With Bitney's support it would be easily enough for an m.a. thesis.

Bitney appeared to be speaking. "One more thing," he said, dislodging something soft and stringy from his molars. "After Christmas break yiv got a new supervisor."

3

The man's name was Cooper. One could often hear his voice booming down the hall from his classroom: "Eros, man . . . Eros and Thanatos," Cooper would proclaim in the voice of a tearful, joyous prophet. A dozen obedient undergraduates would write down the two words, and perhaps later realize they had done so many times before. "The whole thing," he would thunder, "I mean it's all there, man, the whole beautiful goddam thing . . . Eros and Thanatos. . . ."

There was a time when Kvintz had rather liked Cooper: 1968, the post-Bitney era, when they shuffled Kvintz over to Cooper as an orphan is handed to foster parents. The department never seemed to know what duties to assign Cooper. He didn't have a ph.d. so they couldn't let him supervise graduate students or teach seminars. It was rumoured that he smoked a great deal of hashish, so he couldn't be trusted on committees. When they tried to dismiss him, the students marched on the English department and threatened retaliations. So when Bitney was granted a leave of absence they made Cooper the creative writing instructor. Very few graduate students ever took the creative writing course offered; fewer still opted for a creative thesis. Cooper could do little damage there. And besides, when he was a grad student himself at Missoula, he had published a book of long poems. Apparently the poems had a lot of Indian chanting in them. It is true that without the chanting parts they would have been very short poems, but a publication was a publication.

Cooper smelled sweetly of hashish and autumn leaves. On a typical day he might wear maroon corduroys, cowboy boots, a red and gold poncho, and always a gold earring, the kind that reminded one of conquistadors and pirates. When he liked something Kvintz wrote he would write words in the margin like wow! yes! far out! and great!

At first he disapproved of Kvintz's work. He hated "The New Romanians," which he referred to as the "ethnic whutzit." He would call Kvintz in to his office and lecture him on primitive gods, telling Kvintz that his work just wasn't "numinous" or "cosmic" enough. So Kvintz, naturally desirous of having his assistantship continued, found ways of slipping various forms of primal appetites, blood rituals, sun worship, and such things into his writings. The nhl satire, for instance. Bitney had hated it but Cooper thought it had possibilities. In the original version it ended with a bench-clearing brawl in which the referee was flattened.

"It's too . . . too . . ." Cooper strained for the word, fluttering his massive hand, "y'know . . ."

So Kvintz re-wrote it. He made the referee into an over-bearing Cronos figure and the captain of the Maple Leafs into a Zeus figure. His mother, Rhea Armstrong, watches from the stands. The captain beheads the referee in the last game of the winter season and spring returns to the land. He got an A– for this story. Cooper's only comment was to the effect that the "energy was right there, man."

He showed the revised story, with Cooper's comments on it, to Bitney one night in the Strathcona. He even asked if Bitney would take it home and re-evaluate it. The story came back very quickly in the mail. As usual, there was no evidence of Bitney's voice in his critique, only that of a man with a mind like an ice-pick. Phrases like "suffers in revision like an old nanny in a new girdle" and "one winces at the subtlety of . . ." reminded Kvintz of just how much he had detested Bitney. He concluded, "This demonstrates what comes from reading *The Golden Bough* during the telly adverts of a hockey match. One fears the author's imagination has been commandeered by the vulgarians."

Cooper was furious. For a moment Kvintz feared the man would go for his harpoon, a huge rusted affair he had stolen at a Melville conference in Nantucket, which rested in the corner of his office. Cooper's face grew red and his beard seemed to bristle.

"C'mon, Tony," he said to Kvintz, who was too alarmed to remind Cooper that his friends called him Anton. He followed in the wake of Cooper's fury as he strode down to Bitney's office. Bitney looked up from a copy of *Punch*.

"Professor Cooper, how delightful," he said in a casual, mirthless voice. He didn't seem to notice Kvintz.

Cooper, whom no one called Professor twice (he considered it an "uppity" title), seemed to be taking in the detritus that cluttered Bitney's office: the rotting fruit, half-eaten hamburgers and dead flies on his bookshelves; the unpacked books stacked in boxes all over the floor; the unfinished papers, dirty Kleenexes, unanswered memos, and mustard-stained napkins on his desk; the greyish-green pizza that mouldered on Bitney's *Oxford English Dictionary* two-volume set. Perhaps he felt revulsion. Perhaps he felt protective toward Kvintz, who by now had become his protégé. Or perhaps he felt an ancient blood-rage toward this decadent limey and invoked the old war gods of the American Revolution.

"I'm not . . . like . . . into *titles,* know what I mean?" he said to Bitney.

"That's gear with me."

"What?"

"Y'know. Fab?"

Cooper looked at Kvintz like a general in search of his attaché, or perhaps his interpreter. He threw down Kvintz's story on Bitney's desk. "You and your . . . *la-de-da,* horse-buns, piss-ass criticism, you haven't got a schmick in damn-all, you come in here, an man, you haven't even *read* this thing, you come in here –"

"It's my office," said Bitney, picking his teeth.

"Don't mean diddly-shit with me, man, you write your clever little critiques an think you're God's gift to learning – I'll tell you, man, this guy's comin with me, an he's gonna write so far over your head you'll need a thesiosaurus to keep up with him. C'mon, Tony."

Bitney looked indeed as if he needed some kind of guidance, perhaps an Englishman's dictionary of American slang. "Bloozy git," he muttered, as Cooper swept out of his office.

That was the same month Cooper was busted. It was discovered he had been smoking hashish with his American lit class. It was therefore the same month Kvintz was informed that he would be assigned a new supervisor in the fall.

It was also around the time he began his dalliance with Katherine Christine Jones, alias Casey, eternal waiter in the foyer of Assiniboia Hall. At the time, she was twenty, a quietly fervent closet poet who did all her writing in bed.

Then came the new creative writing instructor, none other than Mossy Hogue. One conversation with her and he fell googoo-eyed in love.

He remembers fragments of this sole conversation. He'd asked her how she liked Edmonton.

"Edmonton," she had said, tilting her head and blowing a fern-shaped stream of cigarette smoke at the ceiling. "i live at like the centre/ the sent her/ the sender/ of my own perceptions, you see what i'm saying?"

He said, "Yeah."

When she told him that *she* was the new creative writing instructor, he had gone tongue-tied with joy. He felt as though, when handing her the scuffed manila envelope, he was entrusting his soul to someone. Later, walking home with Casey, he smiled a Kvintzian smile: a fissure opening like a frozen crack in the earth, somewhere beneath a lean bony nose and above a stringy, almost oriental beard. Fate had thrust them together, two northern souls, devout in the holy act of naming, she from the East, he from the West. Later that week, someone claimed she had a beaver pelt on her office wall. Wow.

• • •

Various opening lines have occurred to Kvintz, in the following order: 1) I trust you've recovered from reading my work. 2) Welcome to the wilderness. 3) Hi (followed by a tortured brooding pause), everything . . . okay with you? 4) I've been reading a lot of Proust lately. I hope it doesn't show.

She looks up from her writing, smiles, and the sun irradiates her mass of coppery hair. Her name rises into the sunlight as though proffered by the sun: Mossy Hogue. The sun slips behind a cloud, the office fades into a pale, sickly light.

"sit down," she says, and picks up his manila envelope.

She smiles as she speaks. "the long thing, is that the one bitney hated & cooper liked?"

"No," he says, "the other way around."

"oh," she says, "then, the hockey thing's the one bitney hated & cooper liked?"

"Yeah."

"i see," she says, and the smile remains. An odd smile, one she might offer to her bathroom mirror. It seems to take her importance for granted. In fact, the smile some-how doesn't *include* Kvintz.

"well," she begins, "i read them, & i got this feeling like . . . i have been there before?"

"Yes?" he says.

"all this he-says, she-says stuff, like i have been there before . . . & . . . all these guys with their hockey sticks & this romanian guy brooding over the city in his garret with the canadian flag on top . . . like it's all so phallocentric, do you see what i'm saying? let me ask you a question – can we speak honestly to one another – let me ask you a question . . ."

"Anton."

"anton. what is the subject of your writing?"

"Well, the sketches are –"

"no no, of *all* your writing. everything." Again she smiles and again the smile seems to exclude him. She seems to be looking and smiling at herself across her own desk, as though everywhere she carries her bathroom mirror before her face. "the subject of your writing . . ."

"Anton."

"the subject, anton, is *language*. language. lang/ wage, the wages of the word/ the word made flash/ flash in the mind, in the tongue/ anton/ the tongue unsprung . . ."

"Unsprung?" he says.

"unsprung/ unstrung from the fetters of the colonized mind, unsprung from the pen penis/ the pen *is*/ but i *am* . . . anthony, see what i'm saying, i am . . . i am your reader. do not colonize me, anthony. release me into the yin and yang of your verbal universe, the gulf stream of your labials."

"The yin and yang," he says.

"yes," she says, to the woman in the mirror. "let your jack e/ jaculate &/ let your jill e/ jillulate . . ."

"Come again?" he says.

"a thing i'm working on," she says, and continues to recite.

His eyes wander and rest at last on the beaver pelt he has heard about. But what a bizarre sight. The hide is mounted on what appears to be a large crucifix.

". . . let the nations send o/ vations/ let the nations o/ vulate . . . ."

Scarcely hearing, Kvintz looks out over her shoulder, at the grey November sky, then back at the beaver. He wonders if the beaver wasn't some person in a previous life, a poet perhaps. He falls in love with Mossy Hogue, and one smile, one conversation about writing, and the man is out for the count. Zap, you're a beaver.

Even before she has finished reciting, he knows where he has to go. He has known this, perhaps, for a long time. In a month or two, he will be thirty. He has read the notices. They are dying to hire groundsmen, library shelvers, and keypunch operators. It is too cold to work outside and the thought of spending one more minute in a library is enough to make a man puke.

"do you want these?" she says, holding his stories out to him.

He shrugs.

"let them sit," she says. "wait till they start to lactate."

Kvintz takes the stories, unlimbers from his chair, and leaves.

4

Kvintz trudged and Casey jogged across the quad.

"So what'd she say?" Casey asked.

"Nothing."

"Don't be so grumpy," she said, trying to keep up.

"This department's trying to fuck me around again."

"But what did she say?"

"Ah . . ." he began, waggling his hand in the manner of Cooper, and shrugged. He seemed too tired to respond. Finally he said, "She's got a beaver in there on a goddam *crucifix*."

"I know," said Casey. "I was just talking to her an hour ago."

Kvintz gave Casey an interrogative look.

"I showed her some poems," she offered.

"What poems?" he said, slowing down.

" 'Poems From a Bed,' " she replied. "You remember. The ones you said were florid excretions."

"I said that?"

She nodded.

"Well, I was probably just levelling with you," he said. "I guess I thought you should hear it from a friend before you got hurt."

"I don't suppose you're interested in what *she* had to say about them," said Casey.

"Not particularly," he said.

"You're pissed off, aren't you?" she said.

"I am not pissed off," he said.

"You don't have to yell," she said. "Where are we going?"

"*I'm* going to the employment office."

"Oh, *you're* going to the *employment* office. Yippee shit." She almost lost her temper, but then remembered how positively Mossy Hogue had responded, how she had overflowed with superlatives. Casey had even forgotten to be jealous of her. "I bet I know why you're pissed off. You had the hots for her, didn't you."

Kvintz stopped suddenly and glared down at Casey. "Any dude stupid enough to get the hots for her has got a very good chance of getting deconstructed in her office."

She watched him lope up the steps of the Administration Building, then she turned around and headed for the bus. By the time it arrived she had resolved never to see him again. By the time the bus had reached her corner, she had decided to collect all his books and manuscripts in a box and mail them to him c.o.d. He could keep her poems. She had copies. He could keep them or throw them out. He'd never read them anyway.

• • •

The employment office was in the basement. A lady well past middle years was alone at the desk. She was very wrinkled and her eyelids fluttered, opening and closing like little grey oysters. "Yes?" she said pleasantly.

"You still advertising for a keypunch operator?"

"Why, yes. We actually have positions for three. One permanent and two part time," she replied. "Have you any experience?"

Kvintz smiled, perhaps a little sadly. How many thousands of man-hours had he put into that old Underwood? He'd started six different novels on the machine in the last three years alone. He nodded confidently to the lady.

"It's a computer, you know. Have you had any experience with computers?"

Again he nodded. He'd done a forty-four-page term paper on McLuhan. In a world where all things were relative, he supposed that should count for something.

"And what is your name, please?"

"Anton Kvintz. K-v-i-n-t-z."

"Now, that's an unusual name," she said.

"Oh, most people call me Tony," he said.

• • •

A good ten years after Kvintz got the word from the lady in the employment office, Casey bumped into him by accident. She was coming through on a reading tour and he was helping to host a conference. He'd gained a fair amount of weight and his silvery hair was collar length and modishly parted in the middle. He wore a button on his lapel: Hi! My name is Tony – Electronic Media Resource Personnel.

They went for coffee and he explained that he wasn't at all bitter about Bitney, Cooper, or Mossy Hogue. She had gone back to Montreal and become famous, she told him.

"So I've heard," he said. "So I've heard."

"She's not bad," said Casey. "You should try reading one of her books."

"From what I've heard," he said, "they're real far out, but you know. . . ." He was fluttering his hand the way Cooper used to do when searching for words, fluttering Casey's memory too. Those words. Those people. The way she used to hurry along beside this man. And now – glory be – he was handing her a story.

"You know what I mean," he said.

"No, what?"

"Her kind of writing," he said. "It's . . . well . . . circumscribed by its subject matter. And besides," he added, "it just doesn't lactate."

God's
Bedfellows

The night Rebecca Summers knocked on my door was the
coldest one of the year. I was lying in bed waiting to feel
sleepy. I had just removed my prosthesis, so it meant hop-
ping on one leg all the way to the door of my apartment. (I
have since learned to keep a crutch by my bed for such
emergencies.) I suppose I should have known that only
trouble comes knocking on such a night, but I'm a bachelor. Two things bachelors cannot resist are phonecalls and
unexpected knocks on their doors.

"You must be Howie," she said, and introduced herself.
She looked to be about sixty and spoke with some kind of a
northern English accent. On the shoulders of her tweed
coat was a gathering of unmelted snowflakes. She looked
troubled. "It's your friend, Michael Piggot. I'm afraid he's
had a nervous breakdown."

I was shocked. When I hopped out of the way to let her
in she saw my predicament and showered me with apolo-
gies. From my bedroom I invited her to put on the kettle.

I'd never made tea for a woman as old as my own mother, let alone one from England. I became aware that my apartment needed a good vacuuming. Once I'd attached my leg I decided to get dressed. Our voices carried back and forth through my bedroom door. Michael, she explained, had begun to babble in the staffroom of the school where they both taught. My name and Rickie McAllister's had been mentioned several times. Toward the end of the day, he had fainted; it was all very sudden. She'd had to drive him to the Misericordia Hospital. My boring friend, Michael Piggot, in the mental ward. I could hardly believe it. She had come straight from the hospital. She had tried to phone me, she explained, but the line had been busy. That's true. I'd been having one of those God-am-I-bored conversations with Rickie McAllister.

When I returned with my leg and my clothes on, Rebecca Summers had taken her coat off and was fixing us both a cup of tea. "I could have done that," I said.

"It's no bother."

Rebecca Summers strikes me now as one of those people who is so selfless in her devotion to other people and to causes, that she always looks weary. She was big-bosomed like a robin and had a warm toothy smile that reminded me of cozy English things like cottages and pork pies. She stirred some honey into her tea with a quick efficient motion like someone sketching with a piece of charcoal. Her hands were quite large and none of the fingers arched (as I'd expected the fingers of English ladies *ought* to arch) when she picked up the cup.

"Michael asked if you'd be the one to phone his father."

I nodded grudgingly. Judge Piggot is an imperious old bastard.

"But before you phone him . . . ." She began to fumble in her handbag. "There's something here for you. I think he may have written it today." She handed me a crumpled manila envelope. Beneath the high school logo was my name scrawled in Michael's hand. "I thought if you read it before you visited him perhaps you'd have some idea what's troubling him." "Perhaps" sounded like "praps" and "troubling" sounded like "troobling." I liked her voice. There was a soothing quality to it which made me feel less self-conscious about my unvacuumed floor, my scruffy beard, and of course my newly acquired leg. "Yes, I daresay our Michael could do with a visit," she added with a tired smile. "You'll probably feel a whole lot better once you've seen him."

She seemed to know just how lousy I was feeling. So many crooked teeth in such a compassionate mouth. And to have come out on such a night; it was something close to forty below. She was what Michael Piggot would have called a real cynic's nightmare.

Not that Michael Piggot was ever a cynic. He only pretends to be. He's very easy to get along with, pliable, and charming in his way. He's chubby, his hair dark as a blackboard, skin pale as chalk. He has rather bovine eyes and a jovial mouth, and he's shy in the way that some chubby men are shy; bookish, has a good mind. He reads articles all the time about people like Stephen Hawking and Einstein, stuff that I might claim to have read in order to impress people. He's a math whiz – that's what he teaches – and a tentative sort of a person, probably tentative as a teacher. There's a note of hesitancy in his voice and a virginal bachelor brightness in his eyes.

After Rebecca had left, I turned to Michael's letter. It was done in ballpoint on a very long strip of toilet paper. To make better sense of it I typed it out, but some words and phrases have remained illegible.

Dear Howie,

Did you know???? White octagonal tiles cover floor of men's washroom (upstairs staff lounge) in honeycomb pattern. Good for reveries. EG, stare at one little tile then cross eyes just enough so that tile begins to separate like cell in mitosis. Superimpose split image on next tile so both octagons fuse. Pattern locks into new honeycomb even though subject now slightly cross-eyed.

Aha, you say, what this to do with (something . . .)? Subject having problem with SHOE IN NEXT CUBICLE. Subject bends down cautiously, sees two huge, highly polished black brogues. Winters. Must be, because same grey flannel trousers collapsed around brogues. Indeed, no one in staff of one hundred twenty odd teachers has feet that big.

PROBLEM: Subject has never met Winters, never even *seen* Winters. Principal seen by no one in building except admin staff, secretary. Winters reputed to arrive at work 6:30 A.M., reserves hour between seven and eight for interviews with staff. Tight ship. Only gravest of complaints aired at such an hour. Subject unable to find out much on Winters. Awkward silences. Like asking about Ayatolla in Iran. Simply not discussed. One of subject's students claims P.A. system bugged. Winters monitors everything in every room. Always.

OBSERVATIONS: Subject's bowel incontinent of late, Winters' regular as school buzzer. Observed Winters' shoe several times in last two weeks. Relationship forming in spite of iron cubicles and contemplative silence. Winters always in right hand cubicle. Always grey flannel slacks fallen to ankles, enormous black brogues, highly polished, pebbled toes just visible, 11:00 A.M. without fail. To subject, Winters is presence in cubicle, voice on P.A., figure around whom apocryphal stories accumulate: shut down Hallowe'en dance on account of drinking, shut down noon hour drug trade, poker in study hall. Believes in discipline. Staff meetings short and infrequent, minutes of meetings and Winters' agenda always same, verbatim.

Dear Howie, Do You Get The Point? No?

FURTHER OBSERVATIONS: Recent washroom encounters disconcerting for subject. Brogues so big, no doubts re: owner. Winters next door every time. Subject sees self as monk in cell, faithful to awesome deity. Subject's cubicle repertoire approaches the orchestral. Winters' performance flawlessly unflatulent. Man's control inhuman. Always only inscrutable silence. No grunts, no cigarette smoke, not even rattle of toilet paper roll.

INSTRUMENTS OF OBSERVATION: One coffee mug. On one side, cartoon picaninny, and underneath in florid letters, "Li'l Black Sambo." Mug property of teacher subject is subbing for.

METHODS OF OBSERVATION: Subject holds coffee mug against wall of cubicle and ear against coffee mug. This way subject can detect messages. Jan. 13: "I've been watching you, Piggot. You come to class unprepared." Jan. 17: "Last week in math 20 your fly was at half mast." Jan. 19: "You eat like a hippo." Jan. 20: "Rickie McAllister thinks you're boring." Jan. 21: "Do you know what you are, Piggot? You're a substitute. Do you know what that means? You'll do until a real man comes along."

RECENT OBSERVATIONS: 1) Shoe comes and goes silently. Winters evaporates. 2) Subject suspects he (subject) is harbouring spook inside own body: swelling somewhere under Adam's apple. Won't belch up, just lodges there ominously. Black fiend. 3) Winters spoke to subject for first time through wall intercom today (Jan. 21). Intercom big pink speaker with brown meshed mouth, two nobs for eyes. Winters wants subject to assist vice-principal R. Summers in patrolling halls at noontime. Subject bowed to request as though spook answered from inside. Subject losing freedom of choice, will.

CONCLUSIONS: 1) Intercom is Winters' mask. 2) Winters is God. 3) Winters refuses to hear subject's confessions. 4) Subject must never sit in upstairs cubicle again. 5) Life sad voyage from original warmth to final desolate outpost.

So much for [something . . .] my [something . . .] coffee break.

yr mst hmbl obdnt srvnt,
Michael Piggot, B. Sc., B. Ed.

It was clear to me that Michael Piggot was mad as a shithouse rat. For one thing, why would he write me when he could have phoned me? And why write the damn thing on toilet paper? Perhaps he did the whole epistle on the can. Yet the letter was *in character*. It was almost something the sane Michael would do. I kept wondering, does he believe all that crap or is he being funny? And if life was indeed a sad voyage from an original warmth to a final, desolate outpost, was *I* on that same voyage? I didn't want to go to the hospital. I didn't want answers to questions like that.

Saturday I decided not to visit Michael and all day Sunday I remained in my apartment, keeping the radio up to drown out the sound of the wind. That night I had the following dream. I am standing in the chancel near a pulpit wearing black vestments and a clerical collar, one I picked up during my years in theology school (and which, incidentally, I still have). Michael Piggot is in a bed in front of me, wearing a pair of old-fashioned earmuffs. We are alone. I am explaining to Michael that God, according to Julian of Norwich's medieval doctrine in her *Revelations of Divine Love,* is our mother. All of the facts, even some of the Latin phrases, are right there at my command. I'm inspired. But Michael is inattentive. He's either despairing or yawning or talking when he's supposed to listen. I get angry. Listen! I tell him, take off your goddam earmuffs! He begins to weep. I try a student sermon I wrote on the need for responsible stewardship, but Michael keeps on weeping. I want to comfort him but I can't bring myself to put aside my notes and go *over* to him.

That's all I remember. When I woke up Monday morning I felt even more depressed than I had around the time Rebecca Summers had knocked on my door. I most emphatically did not want to go to the bloody Misericordia. Still, I couldn't put it off. I'd have to phone his father soon and, more than anything else, I owed it to Michael.

I managed to find other things to do until after supper, then I grabbed a downtown bus and headed for the Misericordia. Michael was in the oldest wing of an old Catholic hospital in what used to be an almost exclusively French district. Why Rebecca Summers took him there, I don't know. He isn't a Catholic and he certainly isn't French. I found him in a room with two beds. He lay half-covered with his mouth open, reminding me of a rather pale version of Winnie the Pooh. The occupant in the next bed was curtained in.

There were no bars on the windows, no padded walls, no strange garments with long sleeves in sight. There weren't even any straps on Michael's bed. Of course I didn't really expect these things, but I *did* expect something which would at least attest to the needs of a diseased psyche. A patient walked by the doorway, then another. Outside of looking tranquillized, they seemed entirely ordinary, as ordinary as the card players I had passed in the common room down the hall. Some wore pajamas, some street clothes, some those flimsy hospital gowns. I wondered then if my nervousness at coming here was unfounded. I sat by Michael's bed and touched his arm.

"Michael?" I said, very softly.

I heard a noise behind me, spun around, and beheld the blackest face I've ever seen. A man's face, scarred, peeking through the curtains which surrounded the bed next to Michael. He smiled, menacingly I thought. One tooth, an incisor, was missing.

"*Bon soir!*" he said, still grinning. I nodded politely. I was terrified. "*Ça va?*" he said, and I nodded again. Humour them, the voice of my childhood said. When I

looked back at Michael, he was awake. He struggled to a
sitting position like an animal emerging from hiberna-
tion. I handed him his glass of water. He smiled. The
black man stayed quiet but I had a feeling he was still
watching us.

"Howie," Michael said finally.

Michael was in a pair of maroon and grey pajamas. In
the antiseptic little room they looked garish. He was clean-
shaven, no paler than usual, looking rather normal. Except, perhaps, he was a little thinner in the face.

"Greetings, Michael," I said. "You've lost some weight."
He shrugged and looked somewhat bemused. "You'll soon
be the skinniest teacher in all of Edmonton." No answer. I
wondered what lay behind that bemused look. Resigna-
tion? Serenity? Amnesia? Had I read a madness into Michael's note that didn't exist?

"Well, how are you?"

"Oh, fine."

"I just found out," I lied.

"Yes," he answered with the trace of a smile.

There is only so much you can say to a man under heavy
sedation. I ransacked my head for platitudes and began, as
if in search of props, to case around his room. The black
man was still watching me as though I were the main
attraction in a circus tent. He had gathered the curtains
around his face and in the dim light it looked like a gro-
tesquely fashioned mask of comedy suspended in mid-air.
Again the menacing smile.

"*Veev lamore*," he whispered. I wasn't sure if he meant
love or death, but judging from his expression I guessed it
must have been the latter.

"*Oui*," I said. I was about to take off my parka, which
was damp with melted snowflakes, when Michael spoke.

"Have you seen him yet?"

At first I thought he meant the black man. "Him?" I
asked.

"No," said Michael, shaking his head, looking suddenly

concerned. "Shhh," he whispered and pointed in the direction of the black man. I turned around again.

"*Bon soir*," purred the black man.

"*Bon soir*," I said and this time he smiled at both of us. He obviously bothered Michael in some way. Perhaps he was hiding some hideous deformity. Or had violent tendencies.

"I meant," said Michael softly and slowly, as to a dull student of algebra, "have you seen *him*?"

I looked around but there was no one else in the room. Michael and I were silent. I think I had reached my lunacy tolerance level. I think I was also a little frightened. Not that Michael was about to break into hysterics. Perhaps it was this "him" he referred to. It was as though he was in the room and I was the only one who couldn't see him. Or perhaps it was this bizarre black man, who in some way was obviously getting to Michael.

"You mean your father?" I asked, and Michael closed his eyes and shook his head in a look of kindly exasperation. I suspected he was really living in that final, desolate outpost and I didn't want to go there. Our connection was fading. I just stood gawking. It bothers me to think of it, just standing there like that.

I know we talked about other things in the five or so minutes that followed. The food, the nuns, things like that. He was vague on these matters. It's painful to relate this, but I just couldn't take any more. I made an excuse and left. I'm not sure Michael even heard my excuse. I just hobbled off to the bar.

Last summer I had a serious operation. It began with a pain mid-way between the ankle and knee of my right leg. Shin-splints, said the doctor in Red Deer. This sounded odd to me because I'm not a runner. I've always hated physical exercise of any sort. The pain got worse and they x-rayed the leg. Sure enough, they found a tumor. A biopsy revealed that it was malignant. The specialist in Edmonton told me I had osteogenic sarcoma. The leg would have to go, and soon.

All this involved about half a dozen trips from Red Deer to Edmonton because I was temporarily at my parents' during the summer. My mother doesn't drive and my father's work around the parish keeps him very busy. So Michael, who's always home in the summer, became my driver. The trips were very silent. I was usually too numb to talk about anything. On the last trip I returned to Red Deer with a temporary metal leg, which will soon be replaced by a much more complicated affair. The amputation came less than two inches below my right knee.

I could have had it done in Red Deer, but when I realized I had a choice, I insisted on Edmonton. I didn't mind my parents hovering over me. It was Dad's parishioners I didn't want. Their kind of commiseration was a bland porridge of stoicism and piety which my system no longer tolerates. Michael knows this. His own brand of commiseration is joking about whatever ails you.

One day, after my operation but before the chemotherapy had begun, he brought in an article to my hospital room from *Teentown Magazine* about a young girl whose leg was severed in a car accident. In his quizzical, teacher-librarian's voice he read the following snippet: "When I got my new leg I was afraid no boy would ever ask me out. Now I go out on just as many dates as anyone in my school. And guess what? Now I'm a majorette!" He saw me smiling. He must have known it was my first smile in a long time.

Michael is a bumbler but he knows things. He knows what makes me laugh and he knows what turns me testy. He knows what it's like to grow up loving books and disliking your classmates because they saw you as the classroom scab and you saw them as a bunch of jocky vulgarians and brainless fribbles. I was the minister's son, too short and scrawny to pose a physical threat to my enemies.

Michael was the math whiz who always tripped on his shoelaces. He was fat and the butt of cruel jokes. Of course they called him Piggy.

And now, it seemed, it was my turn to be his comforter. The big difference was that he'd had nothing to do with my misfortunes, and I, with the best of intentions, had contributed somewhat to his. I was the one who lined him up with Rickie McAllister. She likes to save men. She told me that the week I dropped out of theology. She saves them from all sorts of things: despair, loneliness, suicide, masturbation, marriage. She's quite lovely, in a gypsy sort of way, and I thought, why not Michael? He was beginning to look chalky, a thing I've noticed among bachelors who teach school. It seemed a shame. He was obviously lonely. I wanted to give him a sex life. I figured if Rickie could work some of her black magic on him, he'd discover what he was missing. He was a sexual abstainer and I found it annoying. I had begun to find almost any form of innocence annoying.

When I walked into the Strathcona bar, the first person I spotted was Rickie. There she was, sitting with a desolate-looking fellow, Edmonton's own self-appointed Pietà. She was a study in homespun wool and leather. Her shawl was a heavy mauve knit, her skirt a deep purple suede, knee-length boots of brown saddle leather. She was shedding her usual beatific light, this time for the forlorn-looking fellow at her table. His name was Luke. Years ago they had both been panhandlers in Vancouver.

"Michael Piggot is in hospital," I said.

"What?" cried Rickie. "I was just *talking* to him a few days ago."

I began to probe what I presumed was her heart. "It must have been some conversation."

"Why?" she asked, tossing her hair back nervously.

Aiming my words carefully, I said, "He's had a nervous breakdown."

Rickie breathed, "Oh, my God."

"Shit," said Luke, suddenly overwhelmed.

"Are you like saying *I* had something to do with it?"

"Yeah," said Luke, "lay the heavies on her, why dont-cha."

I ignored Luke. "Did Michael say anything strange when you spoke to him?"

"He didn't *say* anything, I told him we should be *friends*, he was making *demands*, he didn't say a *thing*, no expression on his *face* even, he just said, like, 'Hmp' and walked back to his –"

"Take it easy," I said. Whenever the moral spinoffs of Rickie's dishevelled life are revealed to her, she babbles. "I just need to know what happened. Don't panic." Having been the cause of her flap I now began to play the soothing, compassionate buddy.

"Well, you've practically *accused* me of I mean well what d'you *expect*?"

Wisely, I think, she turned to Luke for comfort. He said something I couldn't hear and I lapsed into the same brooding silence I had been in when I joined them. I wasn't even sure what was really bothering me, but I decided it had mostly to do with Michael. Something to do with deserting him when he needed me most. What seemed to gnaw away at me was that I had failed to *talk* to him. Either I was burbling platitudes or he was mumbling about had I seen "him."

Have I seen him.

It was after about six draft that it struck me. Michael didn't mean him; he meant Him. Winters. God.

That letter he wrote in the can must have had its genesis years ago. When I stopped writing for the *Red Deer Advocate* and entered theology, Michael and I kept in touch by having drinks in the Buffalo whenever I returned to Red Deer. It was a club with two members. We called ourselves the Red Deer Wet Set. And he kept asking me if I'd seen God yet. And when I had would I introduce Michael to

Him? Sometimes Michael hypothesized that God was like a mathematical theorem, perhaps one of Einstein's. At other times, He was a fierce old patriarch who called down judgments on Michael and reminded him not to put his elbows on the table.

After seven or so draft it occurred to me that perhaps Michael wasn't amnesiac or mad or even drugged. With his note, he had been trying to revive our old conversation! We could have had a good talk; it could have been therapeutic for him. And like a perfect ass I had walked out on him. I had to go back there. Late as it was, and tight as I was, I had to go back.

I looked up at Rickie. She had developed a disconcerting passion for lugubrious Luke. They were getting rather demonstrative. Up till that moment, I think I must have been holding my head in my hands and looking altogether glum, because Rickie and Luke started getting solicitous about my welfare. I had no time for their silliness. Drunk or sober, I had to get back to the shrink ward. There wasn't a minute to lose. I asked Rickie to drive me to my place in her van and on the double. By now I had a plan. I told them I had to see Michael. Rickie was probably anxious to seem as sensitive toward suffering souls as she always pretended to be. She agreed to drive me.

The three of us left quickly. I don't remember how long it took to reach my place. They waited in the van while I changed. My plan demanded a different outfit. When I climbed into the van Rickie and Luke were in the back molesting each other. They had gone past the preliminaries but fortunately weren't so far into the secondaries as to have reached a point of no return.

"Let's go," I said.

"You took so long," Rickie said.

"Let's go."

"Why do you think it was *my* fault?" said Rickie, brushing her hair in the amber light at the back of the van.

"What's your fault?"

"Michael flipping out," she said, climbing over Luke to get into the driver's seat. "I mean the guy had *problems*. You *told* me he had problems."

"I didn't say it was your fault. Did I say it was your fault?" Sometimes I am such a liar. I must get carried away or something.

She put the van in gear and pulled away from the curb. Luke lit up a joint, which I refused. In a voice that was girlishly contrite, Rickie said, "I bet you think I'm just awful."

I needed a bottle, so I chose this utterance of Rickie's as an in to plead for it. Again, Rickie came through. She drove all the way to her place, got the bottle, then drove me all the way back downtown to the Misericordia. The snow was falling heavily again. I marvelled at how carefully Rickie handled the streets.

"I guess I owe you for the rye," I said.

She said, "Forget it," pouting. "I'm never going to drink alcohol again."

I love it when Rickie puts on guilt. She gets positively Lenten in her abstinence. Maybe that's why she still talks to me. I stir up religious zeal so adroitly. I gave her a little hug. She's always been a sucker for missions of mercy.

Slipping past the reception desk was not a problem. I'd put on my clerical collar and I was boozed up enough to feel the part. The problem was what to say to the fifth floor nurse. I gave her a polite smile and she looked up from the pages of a book. It was written in French. For some reason this startled me. She was thin, sallow, and appeared to be devoid of a sense of humour.

"*Comment?*" she said with an expression of total bewilderment.

"This is station 511?"

"*Bin oui, oeu* . . . yes, but *oeu* . . ."

"Good," I said, and began to limp past her. Walking was painful because, outside, my metal leg had begun to freeze. The nurse called in a restrained voice that suggested to me that she was somewhere between vigilance and respect.

"You needn't come," I whispered, as though I had done these nocturnal visits many times before. "I know the way."

"*D'accord* . . . okay . . . but . . . w'at 'appens . . ."

"*Je reviens tout de suite, comme d'habitude, merci.*" When I read my words in French on this page, they look more fluent than I could possibly have sounded, but perhaps all my disadvantages, my limp, my halting French, my scruffy beard, were factors in foreshortening this conversation. Or perhaps my clerical collar had done its work for me. She began to rise, but did so tentatively. "*Non, merci,*" I added with a humble cleric's smile, "I'll only be a moment."

She looked puzzled, but nodded in return. I turned away and limped down the hallway, proceeding with that benign look I'd learned from my association with so many men of the cloth.

I entered Michael's room. He was wide awake, his night light on. The curtains around the black man's bed were once more drawn. Michael wore that same vague smile. I remember it as a lotus-eater smile: no evidence of mirth, just a sort of blithely upturned mouth as if his lips didn't know where else to go. I closed the door.

"Hello."

"Hello," said Michael, "I thought you might be back."

We stared at each other, Michael rather glum now in his garish pajamas, me in my man of the cloth costume. I had the oddest feeling that I had done this all before but I must have been remembering my dismal dream of Sunday night. The big difference was the bottle. Good old Rickie. Michael had a blue plastic water pitcher, a small juice glass, and a porcelain tea mug. I did the honours, a couple of fingers each of Rickie's *Alberta Shorthorn*, the cheapest most gutwrenching rye on the market. To both drinks I added a little water. Without a word, we raised our glasses and took a stiff belt. It wasn't quite in the spirit of the Red Deer Wet Set; Michael seemed very subdued, as if he were watching TV and I were a boring late show. I can't imagine how I appeared to him in my gate-crashing costume, but I didn't feel unwelcome. I downed the rest of my drink and he did the same. I poured us two fingers more.

Michael looked at me strangely, as though someone had switched channels on him when his back was turned. "Got the word from Albert," he said.

"You got the word from Albert, did you?"

"Yep," he said, "the final word."

"The final word from Albert," I said. "Albert who?"

"Albert Who!" he declared with a sort of mirthless inanity. "To Albert Who!" he shouted, and raised his mug, waving it around carelessly. I cautioned silence with one hand and drank to Albert Who with the other. What the hell, play along. Perhaps, I thought, Albert was his nickname for Rickie McAllister. I'd heard of stranger nicknames.

"I'm lost, Howie," said Michael, again with that mirthless smile playing on his face.

"Lost? We're all lost, Michael."

"Maybe we're all lost," he said, smiling still, "but . . . well . . . some of us are more lost than others." He stared around the room for a while.

"How are you lost, Michael? I mean, are you any more lost than I am?"

"I don't know."

Of course he didn't know. I raised my glass. "To Chaos."

"To Chaos," he said, and we drank.

"To Oblivion," I added, and we downed our drinks to Oblivion, one of my recent visitors. I refilled our glasses. I was still a bit nervous, but I hadn't lost my sense of mission. I assumed Michael would soon get to the central agony and I assumed Rickie McAllister was the name of that agony.

"So you're lost."

"Yes," he smiled calmly.

"Can you explain?"

He nodded and his pudgy face went clenched and squinting. He continued to nod, perhaps for a full minute, then stopped. Methodically he began, "One and one is two."

"Yes."

"Two and two is four."

"Two and two is undoubtedly four."

"And four and four is eight?"

"Yes," again I agreed.

"And eight and eight is sixteen?"

Again, yes.

"And sixteen and sixteen is thirty-two?"

I nodded.

"And thirty-two and thirty-two is sixty-four? And sixty-four and sixty-four is a hundred and twenty-eight? And a hundred and twenty-eight and a hundred and twenty-eight is two hundred and fifty-six? And two hundred and fifty-six and two hundred . . ." Michael continued to rattle off additions like a calculator. I could imagine the computer circuits shooting through his brain, a bell ringing out the totals. Even as a kid, Michael had an envious command of his sums.

". . . eight thousand one hundred and ninety-two is . . . sixteen thousand . . . three, um, three hundred . . . ." The Michael of old, even the ten- or eleven-year-old version, could have gone much higher. He turned to me suddenly and his face was wide-eyed and grave.

"But what if . . . ." His voice tailed off and he began nodding his head again. "What if, um, it wasn't!"

"What if it wasn't?" I said. "What if it wasn't?" I was alarmed. He seemed fearful.

"What if . . . none of that were so? What if one and one *wasn't* two?"

This had me buffaloed.

"Then there isn't anything," said Michael. He looked perplexed, a Pooh Bear who'd forgotten how to get at the honey, forgotten even the existence of honey. We sat hunched at opposite ends of the bed. I looked down at my drink. I could feel the effects of Rickie's rye and Strathcona Hotel beer. "Michael," I said, "methinks you think too much. I wish to propose another toast."

"Another toast."

I was thinking of Michael's pronouncement in his letter: "Life sad voyage from original warmth to desolate outpost." And now he was claiming there wasn't *anything*. There in that mean, square room, I must confess, I could think of nothing. Nothing to toast, nothing to praise, nothing more to say, nothing. I stood up. "To nothing."

"Nothing," intoned Michael with professorial pomp. We drank our whisky down and looked each other square in the eye. "What we have here," he said, "is a very complex problem."

"Indeed," I said, "a very complex problem."

Michael's face crumpled. He began to weep. Except for my dream of him, I'd never seen him weep before, even when we were kids. Judge Piggot had probably trained him out of it. And now it seemed as though Michael didn't really know *how* to weep properly or pleasingly. His face contorted, his breath came in spasms. It made me want to weep too. There were lots of things to weep about, God knows. You just had to look at the newspapers. Farmers going belly up, people out of work, little wars flaring up all over the world. Where was *I* going to get a job? Who'd want to hire a peglegged theology drop-out? I had less than $900.00 in savings. From this beer and whisky funk I was in, a new idea swam down.

"Michael, this Albert friend of yours, was he born in the previous century? Just nod if I'm warm." He nodded and sniffed dolefully.

"And was he a German Jew?" Again Michael, head still bowed, nodded. He was weeping less uncontrollably now.

"And was his name Einstein perchance?" Michael nodded and looked up at me, tearful and snotty-nosed.

"Michael, everyone gets the message from Albert, the final goddam word." I felt justified in putting myself in the same boat with Michael. We'd both recently been in hospitals, we'd both been pretty much losers in love. Michael nodded gravely at my comment.

"Um, do you have a Kleenex, How?"

I gave him one and he blew his nose. What a lift that gave me, seeing him blow his nose. He didn't look like a lunatic. He seemed as ordinary as ever. At worst, perhaps a victim of Relativity Theory overdose. Perhaps Rickie McAllister had only been the last of many straws. Michael used to joke about the Relativity Theory. He claimed it was a hoax to drive professors out of their minds with cosmic uncertainty. I never understood it myself, but perhaps Michael had finally gained a sense of the relativity of things. The fixed universe of numerical truth could no longer sustain the poor bastard. What indeed if one and one were not two?

"Have you seen him lately, Howie?" Michael's composure had returned. He was a bit tipsy.

"Whom?"

"Whom?" he said.

"Yes, whom?"

"Whooooooooom," he said.

"Whooooooooom," I replied. Then I remembered. "Oh, Him!"

Michael managed a doleful smile. I went over to the pitcher and the whisky that sat on the bedside table. I poured us a shot of straight rye. We'd used up the last of the water and I was damned if I was going outside the room to find a drinking fountain. I hadn't forgotten about Mme. Nightingale out there.

"Well, How, tell me."

"I'll tell ya, Mike." I forgot what I was going to say. I kicked off a boot and resumed sitting on the bed. Michael looked more comfortable at his end. He was sitting with his chin on his knees on top of the bedclothes. I assumed the same position.

"Well, Howard, I have seen that bugger. Except . . ." and here Michael beckoned me closer to whisper, "except He changes shape!"

"No shit."

"He changes shape, Howie. One day He sits in the can and listens to everything you say or think. You look around and He's vanished. The next day they give you some pills and He's back. Only He's changed."

"How?" I asked.

"How," he grunted, raising his right hand. This was going to be a long night.

"But how does He –"

"Shh," whispered Michael, and pointed to the black man's bed. The curtains were still drawn but I thought I could hear someone breathing. There was something spooky about those curtains. I half expected the black man to leap out and do something violent and shocking. After a while Michael continued.

"I had a dream, How. I was given the opportunity to view Him," Michael intoned ponderously, "in the mazhesty of His abode."

"In the mazhesty of His abode?"

"Thass what I said."

"Proceed."

"And what I saw was . . ." Michael paused, looking blankly ahead, "the integer ten."

"The integer ten."

"Yes, but ten taken – not to the second power, Howie, not to the third, not to the tenth." He paused gravely. "But Howie, the integer ten raised to the power of one followed by millions of zeros! Billions of zeros. Scillions of em."

I began to feel dizzy. "No kidding."

"Yer goddam rights."

This was almost too much for me. I was reeling.

"I'm lost."

"So am I."

"There's just bugger-all sense out there," said one of us. Bugger-all, said the other.

To sweet bugger-all, we said and our glasses came together with a clank.

I must have passed out on the bed. I could hear Michael's voice at the other end. He was mumbling something about women. I nodded my head now and then, but at first I couldn't open my eyes.

". . . follow the rules, they *know* the rules . . . hm . . . at least I *think* they know the rules . . . maybe that's the problem, Howie. . . . Howie?"

"Mnmh?"

"They don't know the *rules!*"

"Rules?"

"Women! They never *follow* the rules because they've never *known* them."

"What rules?"

"Rules! You know, the things you can't learn mathematics without."

I opened my eyes to see Michael waving his arms like an inspired scientist driving home a point to the academy. He spoke as though I'd been listening on the edge of my seat. "Because, Howie, they . . . *change* . . . *their* . . . *minds.*" He said this very solemnly at the volume of my father's voice when he's reached the peak of a sermon. Then softly, "They change their minds."

"The name Rickie McAllister seems to emerge at this point, wouldn't you say, Michael?"

He nodded gravely. His eyes were wide open but not focussed on anything. He kept nodding until I closed my eyes again. We listened sleepily to the noises of the ward: a doctor being paged in French and then in English, a telephone somewhere that rang unanswered, a steam pipe's muffled knocking on the wall.

"*Pally-vous français?*"

We both jumped. It was the black man; his ebony, scarred head and gap-toothed grin were suddenly presiding. I could see three black fingers clasping the curtains beneath his chin. He reminded me of an old woman on her way to market. I couldn't help wondering if he loved to ambush people like this all the time.

"*Pally-vous français?*"

"*Oui*, of course," said Michael. "Is that all you want?"

"*Bon soir!*" said the black man.

"I'm in the hospital," said Michael. "I'm sick. You can't expect me to go to work if I'm sick." His voice was pleading now, tearful. "It's not like I was . . . lazy."

The black man stopped grinning. He now seemed unhappy and confused. I stood up and poured a shot into a mug which contained his toothbrush. I held out the mug to him. "Take it."

"This for me?"

"Yes."

Very cautiously he reached out for the mug. His arm was plump. He took the mug and raised it to us. "*Salut,*" he said, and grinned shyly.

The effect on Michael was strange. He watched me with a very concerned look. It was virtually the same one he had given me years ago when my mother, in order to combat Michael's fear of dogs, once fed the big German shepherd next door. It worked. The dog and Michael became good friends. And likewise, when he saw the plump arm of the black man, he seemed to be less fearful. I gave Michael and myself another slosh of rye. "C'mon," I said to the black man, and he came. He stepped from the curtains, entirely naked. He had a plump, stubby, child's body, though I would guess he was probably at least forty-five years old. He tiptoed across the floor, hopped on the bed, and hunkered down between me and Michael.

"*Salut,*" he said to both of us, and we drank.

I was a little shocked. But Michael, who on some subjects such as films and books is a bit of a prude, didn't seem shocked at all. He accepted this naked body on his bed in the same way he accepted my clerical costume, without question. So I decided I wouldn't be shocked either. There we sat like three boys playing hookey for the first time. The black man giggled.

"You Michael? I Michael too. Hoo hoo hoo." The two Michaels shook hands. To me he said, "You Michael also?"

"No, I'm Howie."

"You Rev-rund Howie?"

"Yes."

He giggled away. "What you two talk about all the night long?"

"God," said Michael.

"You talk about God?" asked the black man, and broke into a flurry of suppressed giggles. "You talk all night about God?"

"Yes," said Michael gravely, then whispered, "I've seen Him." He said this playfully, as though he was aware of the joke. But I could tell he was serious still. This ambiguity was very puzzling. Michael was acting as crazy as any lunatic, but he seemed to know he was acting crazy.

"I seen God only once," said the black man. His voice sounded Caribbean to me.

"Was it frightening?"

"Oh, no, Not-tat-all, Michael. I only seen His peect-chah."

"You saw a picture of God?" I asked.

"Yes. It was very pleasant."

"You mean a picture of Jesus?" I asked. "With lambs and things?"

"Oh, nonononononononono, Rev-rund Howie, this was God."

"How do you know it was God?" Michael asked.

"Oh, it was God. No doubt-ta-bout it."

"Tell us!" said Michael.

The black man smiled broadly, took a long breath and appeared to be gathering his wits. He took a good sip of whisky. I was feeling rather wonderful. Sort of liberated. Here I was, a man of the cloth, or at least a good imitation of one, sitting in the shrink ward at about five in the morning, boozing with two lunatics, a naked one and my friend. My deranged friend Michael Piggot who listened to the black man as children do, with open mouth.

"I am sitting one day in the school. I am the oldest boy there. Now I help the teacher, she is a big woman name Ruby. She make her own dresses big, special to fit her. Today, she say, we all draw peect-chah. Well the little ones, they all speak at once. One girl she say we draw a tree; one say no, we draw some flowers; boy he say we draw so-jahs in the war; one boy he say we draw God. So Ruby decide, she say okay, we draw God. So this girl say, I gonna draw God's toes. This nex girl she say, I gonna draw God's elbows. An this boy, he goin to draw God's feet. One girl she say she goin to draw God's thing. I tell her God don't have no thing, but Ruby tell me, let them draw God accordin to their own eyes.

"Well, all the children, they go to it. This is nonsense, I say. How they goin to know what God look like if they never seen Him? One little girl, she say: it where you *came* from. I say to the little girl, I came from the south island. Nother little boy, he giggle, an he say, I came from my mother's tummy. We all laugh, an Ruby, she laugh till she shake. Well the children draw an draw till they finish. Then Ruby paste them all together. She call it the composite sketch-o-God.

"I look at the peect-chah an it's funny. None of the arms too big, none o' the feet too small, or the head. All the little sketches seem almost to fit!

"You see, Ruby say, they remember."

Black Michael spread his arms as though emerging perhaps from his plump little belly was a treasure of great value.

"What did He look like?" Michael asked, bug-eyed.

"Well, that hard to describe. But He had breasts as big as watermelons."

Michael Piggot roared and shook, then fell back gasping on his pillow. He closed his eyes and laughed and clapped his hands. He was so drunk (or tired or both) that sometimes the hands missed each other. I think we were both laughing, more or less like Michael Piggot, when the nurse came in. She had someone with her. He might have been an orderly or a doctor. I'm not even sure if she was the same nurse I had confronted at the nursing station.

"Bon soir!" cried Michael and Michael.

They both began to yell at us, she in French and he in English. I tried to answer back in Latin, but the man, who was very big and as humourless as the nurse, ushered me from the room. He hauled me down the corridor to an exit door and I felt too weak to resist. I think I had to hobble all the way down to the main floor because (they probably assumed) I could not be trusted in an elevator. I protested, of course, before and after they pushed me and my coat through the door. In at least two languages. But my words were no doubt lost on those philistines.

It was a while before I found my way to the hospital cafeteria and had a cup of coffee. The waitress was very civil for 6:00 in the morning. The coffee revived and sobered me so that instead of feeling exhausted, I felt almost vigorous. To see Michael Piggot laughing like the Michael of old. That was worth all the despair of the last few days. When the waitress once more filled my cup, she smiled warmly.

"Another long night, Father?"

My clerical collar. It was obviously a talisman of some sort. I thought it strange, though, that Michael hadn't once mentioned it. He knew all about my crisis in faith and my subsequent withdrawal from the college. Perhaps he'd expected me to play the pastor and dress the part. I

was in the midst of congratulating myself on having exe-
cuted some vigorous soul ministry when it came to me that
it was Black Michael who had done the real work. Perhaps
for at least a while, Michael had been rescued from the
wintry outpost of his own mind. And by a total stranger!
He had replaced Michael's fear with something else. A
better illusion perhaps? A better story than I could dream
up? I couldn't help feeling envious.

I tipped my waitress, bundled up in my parka, and
stumbled out into the icy morning. It was still dark, there
was ice fog, and very few cars on the streets. The wind was
blowing tiny siftings of snow from the north and it was
deathly cold. The cars parked on the side streets were covered with a new layer; each one had a little umbilical cord
buried beneath the snow. Even the rich people would have
to take buses today.

When I got to the bus shelter my forehead was frozen
achy and my nostrils freezing closed. The shelter that
loomed out of the ice fog was an aluminum and glass
thing with several panes kicked in. Perhaps the same kids
who had smashed the panes had gobbed on the remaining
ones. Inside were at least half a dozen silent people, all no
doubt on their way to work. They stood still or shifted, like
penguins, from one foot to the other. Only one person had
failed to cover his face with a scarf. All the other faces were
muffled with wool, sending their breath into the frosty air.
No one spoke. It was worse in there than the silence of a
crowded elevator, like standing among sides of beef that
swung in a darkened slaughterhouse. Winter had declared
its primacy over all human intercourse. To break the silence would be impious. This was our tacit article of faith.
It was enough to make one believe that Michael Piggot's
black-brogued God was once more brooding over the scene.

For comfort I went over the flow of events that brought
me here. Rebecca Summers' visit, Michael's letter, Rickie
and her bottle of rye, Black Michael's timely epiphany, and
our meagre victory in the Misericordia psych-ward: Mi-

chael Piggot on his back, eyes closed, laughing from the belly.

I was standing next to the man who had neither hood nor scarf around his head. He was unusually tall, distinguished-looking, perhaps used to driving himself to work. He reminded me of Michael's father but was even taller and more massive. He wore the kind of dark overcoat one expects to see on bank managers or mayors. His lips were set in a grim resolve to endure life joylessly for the rest of his days. Edmonton was in the palm of his hand, you could tell.

I looked down at his feet and sure enough: enormous black brogues. They were encased in black toe-rubbers. At that very instant I wanted to record this man's appearance for posterity. I wanted to put down absolutely everything that had happened in the hospital room, every last detail. It would make a sort of parable, perhaps even one I could live by one day. But how would I end it? Parables don't just dribble on from event to event; they must end conclusively like Black Michael's did. And then it came to me. I would turn to the tall man and yell gleefully and defiantly, *Bonjour*! Scare the bugger out of his morning complacency. I turned to do so.

Before I could open my mouth, the woman beside him said, "Howie?"

She pulled down her scarf so I could see her face – the crooked teeth and bright smile of Rebecca Summers. "You've seen him," she said.

The Father's Love

1

A small black snake with three yellow stripes slides through the clover. It is so hot and dry that things crackle beneath its body. The clover is parched. When the snake reaches the mowed grass at the edge of the clearing it feels vibrations. It stops. Feet are coming. Its tongue darts little flickers of black and crimson. The feet come closer, fat feet and bony feet, feet in sandals, feet in sneakers, bare feet with bandages on the toes. It slips into the saskatoons, moves slowly through the bushes around the clearing, angles off toward the shed. This is the only building outside the circular clearing. It is halfway between the clearing and the lake.

More vibrations. Again the tongue darts in and out. In a tired voice, Rose Pender tells Alex the handyman that something is wrong. It just doesn't *feel* right this time. All that squabble about Rose's cooking. "I'll be damned," says

Rose, "if I'm going to sit around and let Mary Jane bitch and moan about my cooking. She's never done that before. Mary Jane can jolly well get a new cook. Besides, you never heard the girls complaining." A hatchet clatters to the floor of the shed. The snake convulses once and is gone.

Between two new kerosene cans it reappears. It is back within the circle of the clearing, beneath Mary Jane's cabin. Here, too, there are vibrations, soft and musical. In the mellow rise and fall of Mary Jane's voice, the snake coils and waits. Mary Jane is talking to old Mrs. Lamb, who always listens and never interrupts.

"There's too much talk about bombs and unemployment and violence and not enough listening to the Lord," says Mary Jane Meadows, and Mrs. Lamb nods as though Mary Jane has just said, It's a lovely day, Mrs. Lamb. "Negative thinking, Mrs. Lamb," continues Mary Jane. "That's the name of the beast. Negative thinking. Why, Mrs. Lamb, when the sun goes down, would you believe that sometimes *I* of all people fall prey to it? It's *true*."

Mrs. Lamb nods again and smiles vaguely. She is very confused and perhaps just a little frightened. Never in her life has she seen Mary Jane carry on so. She was on the original selection committee that appointed Mary Jane camp director years ago. Beautiful and serene, the ladies had said. A model for all the girls. That was her own first assessment of Mary Jane. She is still a very lovely woman but hardly what you'd call serene. Rose Pender thinks she's got a flask somewhere. When the girls are all in bed after the Hour of Song, Rose says Mary Jane drinks all night in her cabin or takes walks in the woods at the weirdest hours. Ever since her father died, Mary Jane has not been exactly . . . well, you know.

"Mrs. Lamb," says Mary Jane, "can I call you Grace?"

"Of course," says Mrs. Lamb. "Of course, dear." And they are gripping each other's hands.

"Grace," says Mary Jane, "let me ask you a . . . something personal. Have *you* ever fallen prey to the darkness?"

Grace Lamb's heart skips a beat. "Well," she says, "I *do* have my ups and downs, Mary Jane."

"Sometimes I pray for you, Grace. Do you ever pray for me?" Mary Jane is smiling brilliantly, a light in her eyes. Grace has never seen this light before. A great moth as big as a bird flutters in her chest.

"Grace, will you kneel down and pray with me? Right now?"

The cello tone of Mary Jane's voice descends through the floor of her cabin, through the pilings, hums into the two new cans of kerosene, and the snake languidly uncoils. Then there is no humming. The snake passes slowly from the gloom beneath the cabin into the sunlight. A moment later it slides across the path that leads from Mary Jane's cabin to those of the girls. There are four girls' cabins: *Matthew, Mark, Luke,* and *John.* When it reaches *Matthew,* it coils lightly around a tangle of rose bushes. There is a *thunkit, thunkit* sound that jolts the ground. It comes from this first cabin. Inside the cabin is Pud Lacusta. He is waiting for Erna. Against the wooden floor and the propped-open door Pud throws an Indian rubber ball, catches it, flicks it again. *Thunkit, thunkit.* Sometimes he throws it against the clapboard wall and it goes *meadows, meadows, meadows.* He has been told by Miss Meadows that he will not be swimming with the girls any more. It is tough working at a girls' camp, especially when it's run by a bossy old tit like Mary Jane Meadows. He chucks the ball at the propped-open door again and it goes *fuckit, fuckit, fuckit.* Lately he's been thinking how much he'd love to get Miss Meadows. Toss a bees' nest in her cabin at night or maybe put a garter snake in her bed. He flings the ball hard at the door. It bounces out the doorway and down the path.

The snake shudders once. Yellowblack swiftribbon. Gone.

2

Knobby's real name is Roberta. Until she arrived at Camp Serbrojotoma friends called her Bobby. Then at the supper table Pud Lacusta called her Knobby that first evening and it stuck. Erna says he doesn't mean nothing but Knobby's not so sure. She didn't mind though, so she's still Knobby.

She squirms in her wooden-backed chair. She is nervous and hot and has an upset stomach. Soon it will be her turn to speak. She doesn't want it to sound sucky like Shelly's speech. Shelly is so boring.

"I feel I am learning to care for my fellow creatures, for my sisters here at the camp, learning to pray, learning to just let out the joy I feel, um, for all of you here this evening and that is what Camp Serbrojotoma means to me thank you."

Clap clap clap goes everyone and *flap flap flap* go her thongs and up comes Erna to the altar. She's big and brown like an Indian.

"Thanks, Shelly. This is gonna be short an sweet," says Erna, and Knobby claps. Miss Meadows smiles in a way that Knobby has noticed recently. It's as though she doesn't think things are all that funny but she wants people to know she can take a joke as good as the next person. Erna says at night Miss Meadows talks to herself. Mrs. Lamb has a funny smile too. When she smiles, *click*, down goes her plate just a fraction of an inch so you're not sure if you saw them move and maybe they're really her teeth after all and *click*, up they go again.

There is a slow fuse burning through Knobby's stomach. Her mouth is dry. Her speech is folded into a damp little wad in the pocket of her shorts. Some of the girls memorized theirs to make it look as though they spoke like a preacher just as natural as spitting. But so far no one's said a thing about the meaning of the word, and for heaven's sake it's so obvious! Three girls to go before her turn so she's just a-knockin on wood.

Erna says she's glad to see Alex and Pud in the chapel for a change. It should keep them out of mischief for a while anyway. Erna sees that Miss Meadows isn't laughing. Almost no one is laughing. They know if they laugh they'll get looks. Pud just shrugs. His hair's all mussed. He's cute when his hair's mussed. He's tall and he slumps. When he smokes he never looks around to see if someone's looking, he just smokes. He's not scared of anything. He finds out what you're scared of then he drops it down your back. Shelly's afraid of snakes so he chased her with a snake all the way to the kitchen. She went and knocked over the potato salad. Knobby said *she* wasn't scared (half a lie) and he never chased her. Pud likes Knobby, she can tell. This morning he says, hi Knobby, and she says, hi Puddy, and he says, wanna go berry pickin, and she says, not on your life, and he says, I won't do nothin, and she says, that's not what Erna says. He laughs.

She feels her forehead. It's hot. Her mouth and throat are so dry her tongue sticks everywhere it touches. The twinges in her stomach come and go, and when they come they hurt like anything. It's either the heebie-jeebies or the flu. Soon it'll be her turn and no one, knock on wood, has said anything yet about the meaning of the word. People have stopped clapping. Someone hits her on the shoulder. It's her turn! She jumps out of her chair and on the way up unfolds her little speech. She prays that if she gets sick and vomits it'll be after.

"Sisters of Camp Serbrojotoma and Mrs. Pender and Mrs. Lamb and Alex and Pud and Miss Meadows of course –"

"Sweetie, excuse me," says Miss Meadows, "but you should speak louder. Project your voice, dear."

"Oh, sorry."

"That's perfectly all right, dear. I'm sorry I had to interrupt your presentation."

"Sisters of Camp Serbrojotoma and Mrs. Pender and Mrs. Lamb and Alex and Pud and Miss Meadows of course, when I think of what Camp Meadows means to me, I mean Camp Serbrojotoma scuse me –"

"That's fine, dear," says Miss Meadows and gives her princess smile. Shelly refers to Miss Meadows as Mary Jane all the time. Mary Jane is *so* beautiful, Shelly says.

"Um," says Knobby, "when I think of the word Serbrojotoma, it sums up what this place means to me. *Ser* stands for service, *bro* for brotherhood, *jo* for joy in the service of *ma*, that's mankind. In my mind that's what this place means to me."

Erna snickers. That means Knobby's speech *is* sucky. She will kill Erna. She wishes she could change her speech right in the middle. Pud snickers too. He will never want to mess around with Knobby again and she can hardly blame him. She reads the rest of her speech but she doesn't remember finishing. Everyone is clapping now so she walks back to her chair. Her knees are shaking. It was the stupidest speech she's ever heard in her life. She should have said she was sick.

Miss Meadows waits for everyone to be still. She wears a white robe. It's different from the red one she wears for the Hour of Song. Now she smiles and her voice goes flutey.

"Daughters of Camp Serbrojotoma, I want you to share with me the full glory of this moment. I want you to have the will and the spirit and the trust and the joy and all the love you need . . . to glow. Yes, that is right, to glow. To glow like candles in the dark, to glow as girls so that you will glow as women, to glow at school, to glow in the kitchen, to glow with your future husbands, to glow at home with your brothers and sisters, to glow in the presence of your most hated enemies so that you will outshine their hate with your love . . . and *I* would like to glow with you."

She stands quietly before them all. The light has gone funny. The sun is setting and its rays flood in through the altar window behind her. Now there is only the dark outline of Miss Meadows. Someone gasps. It sounds like Shel-

ly. Then someone else gasps and several others. The outline of Miss Meadows lights a candle. As she lights a second candle her eyes sparkle. Mrs. Lamb is handing out
something to all the girls. Knobby feels hers, it's a candle.
She turns around to see if they gave one to Pud Lacusta but
he's gone. The chair next to Erna is empty. Alex is gone
too. Someone dumps what feels like a pillow case over her
head. They're robes, like Miss Meadows' white robe. She
has a long candle in each hand. All around is the sound of
sheets and static, like a hundred people turning over in
bed.

Miss Meadows speaks all silky soft to the girls. "Your
robe is your fortress," she says. "It covers your glory. When
you leave this holy room you must never defile your white
robe until the day of your vows. Wherever you go, you will
wear your white robe in your hearts. It will glow as your
souls glow."

Mrs. Lamb comes up front and nods to Miss Meadows.
All the girls have their robes on and hold their candles
before them. Miss Meadows' voice is scarcely more than a
whisper. "Rise," she says, "rise my little angels, all of you
rise, take up your candle and walk forth, take up your
candle and light it from mine, light it and glow for the
Lord. Who will be first to accept the Lord. . . ."

Of course Shelly is the first to go up and accept the Lord.
As Miss Meadows lights Shelly's candle, she stares into her
eyes and they smile at each other like a couple of angels
discussing harps. Knobby is damned if she'll go up next.
She feels like slipping out the back way and going to bed.
Except it would be dark out. Now Erna's up there. This
pleases Knobby. She outwaited Erna and can't wait to
dump that on her. If Pud Lacusta were there, she would
have outwaited him too. Then he'd know she didn't mean
all that crap she said up at the altar. Erna says he doesn't
beat around the bush, he ups and says, let's do it, just like
that. At first Erna said no, and he said, what's the matter,
you're an injun, aren'tcha? And she said no. She was just

about ready to flatten him then and there, and he said, that's okay. What's okay? Erna said. And Pud said, it's okay you're not an injun, I'm not prejudiced, I'll still do it with ya. She laughed. She said it didn't hurt. She'd do it again.

I'll bet, said Knobby later to herself. I'll just bet it didn't hurt.

3

Mary Jane sits alone at the table in the corner of her cabin. Her left hand is inches from a burning candle, her right holds a fountain pen poised about an inch above a scribbler. The word "no" is printed neatly in block capitals at the top of the page.

"Please," she whispers. "Please."

The pen dips down like the beak of a tiny bird. It prints NO directly beneath the first one.

She has tried talking to him in dreams and she's tried letting go of her soul so that it can float out to meet him while her body remains in bed. Neither method works very well. The dreams are all more or less the same. He calls for his princess, his perfect little princess, her flesh rises to his voice. She's always about ten or eleven, they always end up in bed together. When she wakes up she feels awful, the whole guilt thing all over again. When she tries the second method she always floats her soul into the forest. Sometimes he doesn't show and eventually she just falls asleep. It's confusing because the part of her that's in the cabin falls asleep first and the other part in the woods has to find its way back. Or sometimes he shows and she wants him to hold her. But of course it's her body that's back in the cabin and it never *feels* like an embrace.

The best way is with his old fountain pen and just one candle. She isn't out in the forest floating through the foliage without her body, wanting to be embraced, and she isn't in bed with him sighing and groaning like a bitch in heat, I mean who needs that. With the writing method she sits in a chair, all her clothes on and her soul where it ought to be. And nobody could say there was anything wrong with writing things down. She usually burns the messages afterwards, though, just so no one gets the wrong idea.

People like to pry. He used to say that. It was after her mother died but away before Mary Jane was in high school. *They like to know just what you're doing and they never understand. They'd probably think a father had no right loving his daughter this much, and what do they know about love? Look at all the hatred, look at the divorces.* At the time she had no idea who "they" were. Could he mean the teachers at his school? The kids at her school? Her best friend Nonie Appelgren? It didn't matter. They wouldn't understand, so she tried to hate them all, even Nonie. Sometimes she felt she was only pretending to hate them but later she knew she really did.

That's why this has to be our little secret.

What if Mummy was alive, could we tell her? she asked.

He thought for a moment. *Mummy knows. She's an angel now. She says it's fine. She told me God sent you here for a purpose – so that when Mummy's time came you would take her place. This makes you special, Mary Jane. So special only God should know.*

And Mummy, she said.

He didn't answer. Later, when he was finished, she turned over on the big bed and saw tears in his eyes. His face twisted, his shoulders shook, his mouth opened horribly. *Oh, God*, he cried, *Oh God*. It was awful.

Once she tried to tell Nonie but Nonie wouldn't listen. She cried, Mary Jane, stop it! After that she never tried to tell a soul. She and her father never missed a Sunday in the Temple and never failed to belt out the hymns together. It made the people around them sing louder too. He used to say the louder they sang the better Mummy would hear. She'd just know then. They were there to be cleansed.

"Please," she whispers, and feels something. A warm draught like breath on her back. She smiles as though she is dreaming. The pen dips to the page. ANGELS is the first word.

"Who?" she whispers, "you and me?"

EVERYONE. EVEN SHELLY.

"But how?"

Down goes the pen again. WE CAN ONLY BE ANGELS ONCE WE'VE GOTTEN RID OF OUR BODIES.

She stares at the words. She's been given this message before. Was it once before or twice? Was it here in this very place? Or perhaps at the Summit, where they showed her how to do the writing and the soul travelling. The words are the same, there is no doubt about that.

She carries her candle over to the dresser so she can see his picture. It's a graduation picture, he is thirty-three, it's just before she was born. He smiles as though he wants to do exactly what the cameraman says, almost as though the cameraman were Jesus. She likes this picture. He has such an innocent smile. Beside his picture is a bottle of brandy. She pours a drink, a smaller one this time.

Such a young smile. When he was dying she could hardly recognize him as her own flesh and blood. Senility had set in. *There's so much vileness out there*, he kept muttering. That dried-up old scarecrow of a man wasn't her father, it was the thing that would remain as he struggled to be free of it. And now she could be free of hers. They all could, it was time.

The pen falls to the floor. She spins around so quickly she almost drops the glass. She walks back to the table, picks up the pen, stares at his words. This time she won't crumple and burn the message. Doing so would be denying the words, she's been denying them all along.

No, that's not exactly true. Deep down she has known. Those trips into town, those flimsy excuses. Oh, yes, we burn more of this stuff than ever before, Mr. Danyluk. We have no electricity out there. We're really roughing it, you know.

She ties on her sneakers and walks, one big can in each hand. Over the wet grass she goes. Such a moon, such enchantment. She gets the padlocks for the four cabins. They are all named after men. This strikes her as appropriate, because as she slips on the locks and snaps them closed it is as if *he* is padlocking the doors and she merely watching. When she says never defile your white robe it is *his* voice, not hers.

When she reaches the Hour of Song campsite at the far end of the clearing she lays both cans down, breathes heavily in the moonlight. She has worked up quite a sweat. Gradually her breath comes more slowly. She looks up at the moon, it goes in and out like the beat of her heart. There is such joy in the palpitations of the moon. It makes her forget herself, it sends a warm brandy fragrance through her body. When she lifts her blouse her skin is like rabbit fur. Her nipples rise and burn. She would really love to fling off her clothes right here in the little clearing! Isn't she the silly one!

He will see her, of course. She wants him to be watching. Perhaps he will call for his princess one last time.

Once he said, *No girl should ever be as beautiful as you. It's wrong.* Why? she asked. It made her feel horrible. *Our bodies are loathsome, don't you see?*

Her lips quiver, tears well, the moon spreads out amoebically, still pumping, pumping, with all the insistence of the breathing darkness, the throbbing stars.

"Daddy," she says, and waits. The whole cosmos pumps at her heart with a heaving silver tumescence; the tears stream, silver on her cheeks.

"Daddy."

She stops breathing, her heart pounds into the night throbbing with frogsong, soon the frogs croak to the beat of her heart. They know.

NO.

A breeze caresses her arms, rises, the leaves are clapping.

ONCE WE'VE GOTTEN RID –

"I know!" she cries, almost too loud. She stoops to pick up the first can. As she walks backwards it goes *glug-glug, glug-glug, glug-glug*.

4

In the moonlight the little frogs come up from the lake and hop into the bushes. On its way to find the frogs, the snake pauses by the door of the shed. It is not safe just yet. There are tremors that cannot be ignored. Two voices: Rose Pender's, high and worried, and Alex the handyman's, soft and doleful.

"Big gallon of chokecherry. Strong as hell."

"Oh Christ, Alex. How long ago?"

"Twenty minutes, half an hour. It was right here in *Noah*."

"The whole goddam jug?" asks Rose. "Full?"

"Damn near. It musta been Pud. He knows I stashed it here."

"Alex, if that kid ties one on out here, there's no telling what he'll do. I mean he's hell on wheels when he's *sober*."

"So what am I sposed t'do? Lock it up now that he's stole it? He could be anywhere in that bush."

"Alex, you go and find that little bastard. If he gets into one of the girls' cabins, Mary Jane'll have your balls for book-ends."

"And pray tell what're *you* gonna be doin while I'm out there in the bush with all the mosquitoes, lookin for a needle in the haystack?"

"I'm going to lock up those cabins."

When Rose Pender emerges with a flashlight, the snake darts into the saskatoons. Rose heads for the clearing. Alex's heavy feet pound off into the bush.

The snake heads toward the rising moon. At night the hunting is good. The spiders dance on their webs, the crickets scratch and scratch, the worms flow out of their holes and inch along in the dew. The little frogs come up from the lake.

The snake glides to the edge of the clearing. The trees are silver. The grass and moths are silver. The snake is hungry. It crawls over a dead log and lies in a long wrinkle. Someone walks slowly through the trees but does not threaten the snake. A frog's voice *ribbits* along the dead bark. Another frog hops beside the log from the opposite end. The two frogs are converging on the snake. The flickering tongue knows this. Again the first frog *ribbits* and the second hops on a mushroom just inches from the first. The first frog hops away. Someone's footsteps are getting closer. Slow steps, methodical. The second frog hops after the first one. It tenses for another leap, one that will terminate right on the back of the first frog. But in one convulsion of silver coils the first frog is gone. The footsteps are very close now, the second frog frozen except for its puckering throat. The first frog twitches down the long long tube as the snake glides nestward, away from the slow footsteps. A vile smell rises like a vapour into the night.

The moon is so bright that when Rose returns to *Noah* she flicks off her flashlight. The padlocks are nowhere to be found. On a hunch she walks over to the girls' cabins. Someone has already snapped the locks on *Mark*, *Luke*, and *John*. For *Matthew* she needs the flashlight. And there, too, a padlock hangs from the door. Someone has read her mind. It couldn't have been Alex. She hears a sound that is neither an owl nor a swarm of mosquitoes. It is a footstep away off in the bush. On her way back to check with Mary Jane (since she *must* have been the one to put on the locks), she hears the noise again. One step, then another. It's not the stumbling step of a drunken boy. It could be Alex, going cautious, or Mary Jane herself drinking again on one of those crazy walks she takes. But if Mary Jane was out there tipsy, how would she have the presence of mind to lock the cabins and how the hell could she know that that little shit-raiser was out there with a stolen jug of chokecherry?

She wonders if it's a bear, but it doesn't sound like a bear. The steps are slow and regular like those men who play the bagpipes at funerals. Whatever it is there's absolutely no reason to panic. She marches over to Mary Jane's cabin and taps on her screen door. A light wind passes through her jacket. The wind rises just enough to make the aspen leaves click. She smells kerosene.

Pud Lacusta leans against a tree, oozing the nutty bloom of chokecherry. From here he can see Mary Jane's cabin. Someone now stands at the door but doesn't go in. It's not Mary Jane, it's Rose Pender. Rose heads across the clearing to the cabins. She looks blue and glowing. Now he will go and pay Mary Jane a little visit. He will give her door a kick and say boo. Then if she starts bitching he will give her some sass. He will say have a drink, y'old bitch. He will piss on her floor.

But she's not in her cabin, she's nowhere. He sets the jug beside the burning candle and sits down heavily. He reads a note that begins NO. NO. ANGELS. EVERYONE. EVEN SHELLY. More of her Jesus glow talk? It doesn't make a bit of sense. He takes a pen and tries to draw a cock and balls on Mary Jane's *Triumph Over Temptation* booklet. His hand slides all over the place, it feels numb. He grabs another pamphlet, it's got things underlined, it talks about the Chokmah of this and the Geburah of that. *The 22nd path, from Malkuth to Yesod, is fraught with peril.* He likes that phrase, "fraught with peril," and repeats it out loud. *To see a figure in a scarlet robe,* he continues, *means that you have strayed. This is the path of Saturn. This may be the Beast Himself. Beware.*

He goes back to the note again. It says, NO. NO. ANGELS. EVERYONE. EVEN SHELLY. He reads the last part out loud. " 'We can only be angels once we've gotten rid of our bodies.' "

Pud Lacusta looks up. Something is wrong. Spooky. He grabs the jug and lurches for the door. He stands in the doorway until his mind stops going on about things, then he stumbles out into the night. He can see the cabins in the moonlight. No one is in the clearing. He thinks he will give Erna a visit. She's in Knobby's cabin. Maybe he will give Knobby a visit. He lurches into the trees and stops for another tug. An owl hoots. Some footsteps, coming slow. Maybe it's Erna, maybe it's one of the girls out for a good time. A good time with Yours Truly. He heads for the sound. It is coming from the edge of the clearing. He stumbles on a root and the jug goes flying, but it doesn't break. He kneels down by a big clump of bushes to pick it up and hears a high voice on the other side of the bushes. He weaves through the bushes until he sees her. She is bending over and walking backwards holding something. There is no one else around. She sings a song like she was playing by herself in the garden.

> *Be careful where you put your little feet little feet*
> *Be careful where you put your little feet little feet*

It's not Knobby and it sure as hell isn't Erna. It *sounds* a bit like Shelly. He decides it's Shelly. Shelly thinks she's such hot stuff. He will show her a thing or two about hot.

"Shelly! Hey, Shelly!"

She straightens up. She's holding something heavy.

"Shelly put yer belly up to m -"

She turns and looks at him. She is not Shelly. She is someone he knows. She is smiling funny, oh Jesus. Snarls and spits.

"Here of out ass filthy your get you!"

The jug goes up in a slow silver spin as he falls back

into the bushes, he's up and running slow and shriek, he runs faster, faster than the yelling voice pursuing him, he runs through the trees till he knows the long high scream is his own voice. When he stops yelling it stops yelling.

• • •

For my love I make a perfect circle. We will all glow in a perfect circle. We will dance before His radiance.

5

Returning from the backhouse in the dark is no big deal. You just follow the path and when you hit the fork you keep right. *Luke*'s the first cabin. But the first cabin has a padlock on it. What in hell's goin' on, Knobby wonders. She looks at the cabin and in the moonlight it doesn't look quite right. So off she goes down the path and *Matthew*'s got one too. Some retard has gone and locked her out and all the others in! She tries to remember. This has never happened before. There's never been locks on the doors. Something is wrong, bears or something. Unless Miss Meadows is locking someone in for some reason, like Erna. She knows about Erna and Pud, Erna said so. Does that mean Pud hangs around out there?

She wonders what it would be like to neck with Pud, just neck with him. Erna would kill her and Erna's her best friend. Besides, Pud Lacusta's show-offy. He's loud-mouthed and he chases girls with the yuckiest things he can lay his hands on.

Knobby goes back and does a circle around *Luke*. Its windows are too high to break into and she'll be damned if she's going to up and holler for Miss Meadows. She minces around her cabin again. She hears someone walking through the bush. Or something. It walks slow, like an animal grazing. It's far enough away that she's not scared.

She taps on the door. "Erna," she whispers, then knocks louder. "Erna!"

Someone is coming to the door. Erna's voice, heavy with sleep, says, "Pud?"

Knobby nearly splits a gut. "No, you retard, it's me!"

"Knobby?"

They rattle the door, whisper and chuckle. Erna says to Knobby, get a piece of wood and pry it. Knobby goes at the latch with a garden stake. The stake snaps. She whispers this to Erna and hears a cabin full of girls giggling. This is the best audience she's ever had. Then she hears no more giggling and she knows that it's up to Erna now. She tucks her nightie round her knees and listens to the sounds of crickets and frogs and owls. At least the twinges are gone. She feels okay now. There is another noise in the bushes. One foot, then another. It's a creepy sound. And a smell that comes in with the breeze, a strong smell.

A commotion inside the cabin makes her leap to her feet. A horrible thud like someone falling to the floor. It comes again and everyone inside is laughing and screaming. Again the thud, it's against the door. She knows this must be Erna. Erna's big powerful body crashes at the door, and each time, the padlock does a little dance. But it's no use. Knobby tells Erna she's going to tell Miss Meadows.

This is so no one will panic. She'd rather sleep in a tree than talk to Miss Meadows now. She'd think Knobby's been out fooling around. She'd make Knobby read the pamphlet. That's what Erna had to do when Miss Meadows found out. *When we have our various lusts we must learn to drive them from our minds. We should think about the good things in the Scriptures. We should jot down a specific example of something good to think about from our lives.*

Barf.

Knobby hobbles and hops along the path to the shed. There's an old cot in the corner for Alex to nap on. There's no lock on the shed. She can't see a thing, she's cold. If she moves toward the cot she'll probably stub her toe on the tractor mower or something. She waits. Is there a blanket on the cot? She can't remember. Slowly she moves across the floor. Her feet feel things, potato sacks, newspapers, oily rags. Her hands feel a vice on the workbench. She can see where the moon shines through the door and the window. She can see the tractor mower. She touches the cot. There's a blanket. She's shivering. She wraps the blanket all around her and lies down. She's not scared. She shivers. But who wouldn't shiver.

In through the door so loud and shrill, a scream. A scream she's never heard the likes of. And running. She freezes to the cot. Bears, she thinks.

The scream brings Grace Lamb out of a dream. "Mercy!" she whispers, and then, "Jack, Jack!" But Jack is dead and she remembers where she is. In the dream Jack turned into Mary Jane's father, what's-his-name. He was somewhere in the forest. He looked old, the way he looked that last time Mary Jane brought him out here.

She listens for another scream, breathing in all the dread in her cabin, breathing it out. Again the great moth flutters in her chest. When her heart stops pounding so fiercely, she will tiptoe across her cabin floor and light her lantern. Then she will fix herself up a bit and put in her teeth. If she has to die in her bed at least she will look presentable.

Things at the camp have gone too far. They have simply got out of hand. First it was all that nonsense of Mary Jane's about the dark. She's just getting too overwrought. She'd have to talk to the committee about Mary Jane and it hurt her to think about it. All that candlelight hocus-pocus, it's just too . . . too *emotional*. She must have picked it up when they sent her down to that Summit place in Malibu. From what Grace hears, any time one of their people goes down to that Summit place they're never quite the same again. And Mary Jane's father ups and dies the minute she's gone to California. It was too much for her. All that Malibu hocus-pocus and then a death in the family. And the two of them so close and all. Mary Jane knows how to treat her elders. (Young people today can't wait to wash their hands of them, can't wait to ship them off to an old folks home.)

But enough is enough. Now it's screams in the night. You can't tell Grace Lamb this is a place to send God-fearing girls. Lunatics running around at all hours. She'd have to talk to the committee first thing next week. It was a painful duty but enough was enough.

She tiptoes over to her lantern but hesitates. If she lights it, whoever is out there will *know*, and might even come and get her. But if she stays in the dark, maybe he will go away. She hears the sound of running feet. They gallop right past her window and out across the clearing. She can taste the dread of it like metal in her mouth. She stands and clenches her toes on the cold linoleum and wishes to God her Jack were alive. He wouldn't stand for this nonsense. Why she should confuse Jack with Mary Jane's father, the good Lord only knew. Mary Jane's father was such a crotchety old thing. He didn't like Grace's Prayer for Peace. He said, *Let them drop the bomb. So much vileness out there, nothing's worth saving any more.* Mary Jane was mortified. She took him home a day early.

Knobby holds the hatchet so the sharp part faces her. She's not afraid to use it but she's not going to go chopping someone's head off. She waits on the cot. Whoever's there just stumbles around outside. He groans like a man. He's puking. It sounds like he's dying, like someone went and ripped his guts out. It sounds like he'd rather be dead. She wishes Erna was here. Erna'd go out there and tell him to go puke somewheres else. At least he hasn't picked *Noah* to get sick in. He goes *crash* against the woodpile and starts swearing. He's coming this way. He stumbles in the door and knocks over the rake. It's Pud Lacusta, he looks awful. He heads for her, staggering.

She cries, "Just what in the Sam Hill you think yer doin?"

"Aaagh!" He falls back over the tractor mower. He didn't even see her on the cot.

She says, "You wanna get sick again, you go outside."

"Watch out how you wave that thing around, Jeez."

"I'll wave it around as much as I feel like."

"Okay!" He scrambles to his feet and leans against the wall. "Where am I anyway? Am I in *Luke?*"

"You're in *Noah.*"

"*Noah?* This is *Noah?*"

"Look around."

He stumbles around, mutters things and swears. "Where'm I gonna sleep?"

"You got your shack."

"Yeah, great. That bitch Meadows, she's out there. She'd come . . . I think she wants to kill me. She's fuckin crazy." He falls to his knees, he's wiping his mouth. "Scratched my face," he mutters and starts to swear again.

"You can sleep on them potato sacks," she says.

"Thanks for nothin." He collapses on the sacks and starts to moan. He stinks of hooch and vomit. Pretty soon he's only talking to himself. There's no more noises outside. He goes to sleep. It's getting light out. She can see scratches on his arm and his cheek. His hair's fallen over one eye and his face is perfectly still. He looks nice like that. It would be a shame if he moved or if anything changed and he didn't lie just like that on the potato sacks.

Knobby yawns. She knows she has to do it, she can't stop herself. She gets off the cot and takes the blanket and covers Pud Lacusta.

The snake cannot enter the clearing, it goes around and around but the fire is always there, licking away at the dry bush, it gets higher and higher. The snake's nest is inside the circle of fire, it keeps trying to find a way in. The heat is too intense. It angles off into the bush, weaves through a thick stand of willow. It emerges into the pale light by the door of the shed.

Inside Knobby stirs. She's chilly. She smells smoke. She has just been jolted by a dream. She dreamed she leapt through fire with this boy who snores on the floor. There is blood on her nightie, real blood. She reaches down between her legs and dips her fingers in it. Real blood.

Protection

"Schmuck, you tell me to get behind Wiener, I get behind Wiener, so *pass* already. I was in the clear!"

"In the clear yet, you call that in the clear? The time you take getting behind Wiener I could change my socks and underwear!"

That's how I remember Pinsky during practice, putting Segal in his place. Segal, already an angry young man ten years before his pilgrimage to Allen Ginsberg, already tortured by dreams of glory, the victim of a body too long and spindly to give any quarterback confidence in him. Pinsky, perpetually venting his rage on boys a head taller than he was. Segal stalks away from Pinsky on his fourteen-year-old giraffe legs, and Pinsky lopes back to the huddle, spits on his hands, claps them twice. A new scrimmage is seething to be born somewhere beneath his brush-cut.

And I remember a boy almost fourteen himself, a gentile, though not yet conversant with that word, sulking as he stood on the curb of Westminster Drive. He wanted to play, too, but he thought these Jews should ask *him*, and he was angry because they found him so easy to ignore. He rubs a spot beneath his nose where the peach-fuzz itches, like his body, to proclaim his manhood, the spot where my moustache now grows. I remember his goyish rage, less volatile than Pinsky's, less frequent than Segal's, but rage all the same. He is thinking *If my stupid parents had been satisfied to keep our old house I'd be playing end both ways on Carpenter's team and not hanging around this stupid neighbourhood the only unjewish kid my age on this crescent and if my brother's stupid friends hadn't chased Alvin Pinsky into Mrs. Bercovitz's backyard I'd be out there now even if I wasn't Jewish and if I was in high school with my brother I'd be playing in a real league not just a stupid pick-up league.* But he knows that beneath all his excuses for not playing that day is the fact that he, Drew Edmond, the only non-female gentile his age on Westminster Drive, has laughed at Alvin Pinsky.

Less than a month before, it was Pinsky, not Drew, who'd wanted to play. I can run, I can pass, I can kick, said Pinsky to Drew's brother Hank. Hank was quick-witted, tall, built for speed, and sixteen. I can catch, Pinsky continued, I can call signals, I can block. You just don't *say* that to Hank or his friends. They're all sixteen and they play in a high-school league. You just don't go shooting off your mouth at those guys, because they don't take anything from anybody. You learn to ask questions if you're younger and smaller, and wait to be invited. Drew Edmond knew that. Anybody with any brains knew that. And you *especially* don't go shooting off your mouth if you're wearing a brand new pair of *red* running shoes. Pinsky was dead before he opened his mouth. It was Hank who coined his new name, Little Red Running Shoes. They all roared as though they'd learned how to laugh from watching cowboy movies. You know, the tenderfoot comes into the bar and orders milk? They knew Pinsky was what they called a hotshot and they weren't going to let him off easy.

I remember Pinsky better than I remember anyone in that neighbourhood, and yet I always despised him. He looked to me like a shrunken version of Jerry Lewis, except his voice was perpetually hoarse from yelling, and his functional range was usually somewhere between fervid self-absorption and hot-headed rage. He was a small boy at a time when all boys wanted to be able to hold their own in rough company. I'm sure he had all the attendant small-boy complexes too. He over-compensated for his size in many ways: he practised his foul shots under the hoop on his garage for hours, he trained for running with a stop-watch, like an Olympian. His mouth seemed twice as sharp and loud as anyone else's in junior high. And though my brother's gang had chased him into Mrs. Bercovitz's back-yard, ridiculed him with impunity, no one in junior high ever picked on Alvin Pinsky. He was street-wise and had bodyguards. And they were almost always gentiles. He had lots of Jewish friends who could have done the job, I suppose, but with Alvin's runt instinct for survival, he must have seen an advantage in keeping on good terms with the non-Jewish warriors in the West End.

One such warrior was Artie Hrynchuk, a big freckled boy from one of the poorer neighbourhoods west of my new home. He was a good-natured fellow, but very tough when he got in a corner. Only now do I begin to understand how Alvin Pinsky curried favour with Artie Hrynchuk or other boys like him. I've heard how in prisons vulnerable boys dispense sexual favours for protection, and in mobs how money buys the same commodity. Perhaps no boy near Westminster Drive knew better than Alvin Pinsky that nature's cruellest laws of survival held sway even there. It was the most swaddled neighbourhood a boy could grow up in, but it was not immune to the inevitable. And knowing this before any boy should have to learn it, Alvin Pinsky sought the currency that would protect him from bigger boys. Not only street gangs or punks from the outlying areas, but smart alecs like some of my brother's friends, or practical jokers like my brother; boys who might rob Pinsky of his fiercely guarded runt's dignity.

For Artie Hrynchuk, the currency was Jane McKernan. Even without those precociously huge breasts she would have been considered good-looking by our standards at Buckingham Junior High. But her dad owned the Edmonton gravel pit and she was taboo for Artie, who lived with his mother in a shack down by the river flats. Alvin Pinsky, who listened carefully and collected confessions like a prurient priest, soon found out about Artie's burning passion for Jane McKernan. She had lived next door to Pinsky for many years, grown up with him. And because he could make her laugh with his imitations of Jerry Lewis and Bill Haley and Elvis, she had a great affection for him.

So before he had the slightest idea what go-between meant, Alvin Pinsky became one for Artie Hrynchuk. He must have been pretty good at it, too, because before long the three of them were seen smoking cigarettes on the river bank and heading out for sodas at the Pat. Then it was just Artie and Jane. And finally, when Artie's case had been argued at home to the dour Mr. McKernan, Artie's half-ton could be seen parked on Jane's driveway nearly every night of the week. Artie never forgot it and no one laid a hand on Pinsky when he was around.

There were plenty of bullies at Buckingham Junior High, fights during the noon hours, and little pockets of anti-Semitism of which I was only vaguely aware when I was thirteen. Almost no one I knew would call somebody a dirty Jew. Somehow, such an insult never produced the potent sense of release that you got from swear words that have their origins in scatological or genital lore. And among the parent generation of relatively wealthy WASPs, what anti-Semitism did exist was disguised as something else. At thirteen, it never occurred to me to interpret the use of the verb "to jew" as an index of anti-Jewish sentiment.

It was punks and troublemakers (we called them "zoots") who used racial slurs. When Bunny Fillion called

Segal's sister a dirty Jew, he got five on each. When I told my grandmother about the incident, she told me she felt sorry for boys like Bunny Fillion, who were too ignorant to realize that Jews are no worse than Chinamen, Indians, or Bohunks. I'm sure now that Granny didn't feel the least bit sorry for Bunny Fillion, or for persecuted minorities for that matter, but I'm equally sure she didn't know it.

I didn't play that day I watched Pinsky put down Segal, or that week, or any week in July. But when the Asiatic flu hit in the first week of August, and kids my age clear across town were running fevers for as long as three weeks, my luck changed. I, Drew Edmond, was the first kid on the block to get the Asiatic, and when Alvin Pinsky's team started to get decimated by it, I was all better. The word must have got around. It wasn't Pinsky who came to my door, of course. It was Marvin Fuchs and big Al Rudnunski. They didn't have to explain things. I knew why they were there. I even forgot to get proud and play hard to get. Big Al let Marvin Fuchs do the talking. This was more than a dozen years before Fuchs had his PH.D. thesis accepted at Columbia, but even then he was a word wizard. In fact, he was the most pedantic thirteen-year-old I ever met, but so good-hearted and considerate that many of the boys I knew could eventually forgive him his intellectual superiority.

"Drew," he said, and looked me right in the eye as I stood halfway out the door of the back porch. "Due to an oversight . . ." and right then Al Rudnunski laughed nervously. I think I laughed too. "Which is to say, ah, Alan and I and a good *number* of our, ah, teammates . . . think that you'd make quite a strategic addition to the, ah, team." (If you don't think a thirteen-year-old kid would talk like this, you didn't know Marvin Fuchs.) He stopped. A joke and a grave concern for propriety were warring on his face. The joke won out: "Especially now," he said, and we all laughed.

The first game they played I dropped a Pinsky pass in the first quarter that was right in my arms. Wiener told me I needed someone to kick my ass for me. But in the third quarter I grabbed an interception and ran it down to the Oliver team's thirty-yard line. Segal hugged me so hard I was afraid he was going to kiss me or something. Even Pinsky clapped me on the back.

So after victims of the Asiatic started to trickle back from their sick beds, Pinsky kept me on the team. I wasn't that fast or that big or that tough, but I could catch passes and I didn't try to tell Pinsky how to run the offence. I, Drew Edmond, was the only gentile on the team, so I felt flattered to be kept.

Our games were arranged *ad hoc*. Whenever he heard of a team in the West End, Pinsky would phone someone and the game would be set for Sunday because Pinsky's old man didn't want him playing Saturdays. According to Jane McKernan, the Pinskys were kosher. I didn't know what that meant but I was too self-conscious to ask her. My conversations with her were always brief because I was so much in awe of her breasts and embarrassed by my fascination.

We weren't a bad team. We won our first game and lost the next two by close margins. But when, in late September, we beat the team from J.P., we were astonished at what appeared to be our prowess. The J.P. team was big and tough. Some of their guys were older than us too, and you could tell by the way they dressed and smoked that they knew what life was like on the wrong side of the tracks. Perhaps we allowed ourselves to forget that while we had eighteen players, enough to sit six on the bench and relieve the tired ones, they came with only eleven players, one short of a full team. And Ernie Kobluk, their tough fullback, had to watch from the sidelines with his arm in a cast; he'd been fighting again. And Bunny Fillion was down in Bowden serving out a short term for car theft. And the Asiatic had sidelined Shag Muler, reputedly the toughest kid in Buckingham Junior High. Looking back, I'm sure that's why we won. We beat them by two touchdowns.

Though I took scant notice of it, there was some bad feeling at the end of the game between Al Rudnunski and Vernon Kiss. I'd known Kiss since I was seven or eight. He was the only rich kid on the J.P. team, big for his age, and pushy. He had a smile that never spread beyond his angular feline mouth. Like Alvin Pinsky, he travelled with tough kids from the meaner streets of West Edmonton, but unlike Pinsky he really was mean. I saw him pick on Marvin Fuchs before Marvin grew up and filled out solid. I knew that Vernon could take me in those days or I would have lambasted him when he beat up Marvin.

I noticed, too, at the end of the game with J.P. when the shoving started with Rudnunski, that Vernon had not exactly undergone a moral rehabilitation in the intervening years. I'm not sure why he picked on Rudnunski. Maybe because Big Al was such a gentleman. We all liked him. He was smart as a whip but he disguised this with his self-effacing manner and the jokes he made about his own fatness. He could have handled Vernon but he chose only to push him away.

"C'mon, ya candy-ass little kike!" Vernon said to Al, and we were suddenly quiet. A funny thing to say, too, because Rudnunski was neither little nor in retreat. "C'mere!" Vernon snapped. Al was right there, immovable at that moment as he had been at right tackle during the game. Immovable as he was to be eight years later when he quit his last year of law and joined the Israeli army.

We all moved in close. First, one of the smaller guys from J.P. tried to calm Vernon down, but he was adamant and he hurled his teammate back. Then Kobluk came between them, solid as an oak tree and his arm out of the cast now. Vernon backed off. He respected Ernie like a fox terrier respects a bull terrier. Ernie was smart enough to know that eighteen to eleven was not comfortable odds. Their team gradually moved away and not a blow was struck.

Perhaps it was more pride than masochism on Pinsky's part that made him accept a return match from the J.P. team. Their captain phoned up Pinsky and seemed friendly enough. Pinsky, not one to let the safety of his troops get in the way of his pride, accepted.

"You crazy little putz, why?" asked Segal. We were all lounging in the shade of Pinsky's garage.

"So why not? This time it's at Glenora School. Neutral ground, like."

"I don't know," I said, but I wouldn't say any more. I don't remember if I was afraid or just trying to be sensible, but even to appear the latter would have been interpreted by Pinsky as cowardice. He riled me many times, but Pinsky was no coward. Perhaps Stanley Segal feared Pinsky's reproach as I did; he didn't argue much with Pinsky after his initial outburst.

"We can get Hrynchuk this time," said Pinsky.

"Are you crazy already?" said Wiener. "Hrynchuk told me he's starting to work weekends. Sundays yet. Besides, he's from J.P. If he plays for anybody it'll be for Kobluk."

"Ix-nay," said Pinsky, and spun the ball straight up in a spiral, caught it, spun it up again.

None of us asked what this talk about Artie Hrynchuk was all about. It was like asking your sergeant before a raid if you thought the platoon had a snowball's chance in hell.

"Hrynchuk's in the bag," said Pinsky, and suddenly, with another game against J.P. looming four days off like a thunderhead, I got the feeling that Artie Hrynchuk had become our protection as well as Pinsky's. I imagined Hrynchuk in ways that I would have imagined the Lone Ranger a few years earlier. We had no doubt at all that he could handle Vernon Kiss and Fillion. Once he'd even taken on Kobluk and come out on top. But could he handle Shag Muler? Maybe. Muler was a tall, bony, hatchet-faced boy. His feats as a warrior were passing into legend. We didn't hate him, but there were times we feared him.

When we arrived on our bikes for the game Sunday afternoon, Hrynchuk's truck wasn't there. What made things worse was that their team had all its big guns back. Bunny Fillion was fresh out of Bowden, smiling around a broken set of teeth, exhorting his friends. Muler was there, hanging loose and smoking like men I'd seen in gunslinger movies. And Butch Bullmer, who just stood around taut and low to the ground, solid as a fire hydrant. One of the St. Denis brothers, smoking in a white shirt with the collar up and wearing a pair of zooty pants, and the other St. Denis brother combing back his ducktail. They must've had almost two dozen guys there and they looked more like a hit squad than a football team. Most of us had football sweaters and a couple of our guys even wore shoulder pads. But most of the J.P. guys wore black leather shoes or boots and not one of them had a football sweater. I assumed that in J.P. they considered running shoes or football sweaters to be sissy. It never occurred to me they couldn't afford such luxuries.

There were several guys from J.P. I'd never seen before, and when we'd tossed the coin and begun heading to our end of the field to kick off, one of them came with us. I asked Marvin Fuchs who he was but he had no idea. The newcomer seemed to move with a certain authority for a small fellow. He was thin, pale, and otherwise nondescript: a scruff of hair the colour of dust, no eyebrows, prominent cheekbones that made him seem hungry, small pale blue eyes that took in everything.

"You know him?" I asked Segal in a cryptic whisper. Segal only shrugged. "Well?" I persisted. Segal pinned the ball for Irwin Wiener, our kicker.

"Get onside, Drew," said Segal grimly, and then, "No. And that's the whole point, see?"

No, I didn't see. I looked over at the new fellow once

more. Instead of running shoes he wore light-blue socks
that seemed a couple of sizes too big for his feet. He had no
football sweater either, just a white T-shirt and a pair of
baggy jeans with a red strap on the left thigh, where car-
penters hang their hammers. At our school it was a tradi-
tion that no one wore a red strap unless he wanted it torn
off at noon hour. This fellow didn't seem bothered about
that. His jeans were faded, so that red strap had obviously
remained unviolated for some time. I couldn't get a fix on
him. There was something ancient and aloof about him,
though he was probably not much older than we were. I
remember thinking, as big Irwin Wiener raised his hand
above his head like real kickers do, this new guy has never
been in a classroom. Even more than the invincible Muler,
this fellow struck me as belonging to that world beyond
my neighbourhood where boys didn't have mothers and
men slept on the river bank and smelled of lemon extract.
It was the hungry mouth and the watchful eyes. I thought,
What's Pinsky up to now? Is this a stray his mother feeds?

No one scored in the first quarter. Kobluk made some
first downs on us through the left side of our line, but every
time he tried the right side Rudnunski stopped him cold.
Their quarterback could throw, but we had guys like Wiener, Segal, and the new guy who were tall enough or fast
enough to knock the ball down. We didn't get any inter-
ceptions, but they couldn't connect with their long passes.

Offensively we were almost nonexistent. Pinsky tried
passes, but they rushed in and either knocked them down
or sacked him. They were hitting hard, very hard. Pinsky
got nervous, and we started fumbling on the hand-offs. It
took us a whole quarter to get our bearings.

Then their quarterback started connecting and Kobluk
started knocking a few heads around and they scored twice
and missed both their converts and we scored once when
Pinsky ran back a kick almost the length of the field. It was
12-7 at half-time.

I was sharing the water jug with Rudnunski. He just sat in the grass and looked battle weary. Vernon Kiss and another guy had been double-teaming Rudnunski. They'd been slugging and kneeing him and he hadn't been saying anything about it. He just sat there big and sullen. Finally he said, "They're out to get us, Drew."

"I know," I said. "But we can dish it right back."

Rudnunski shook his head. At first I thought he meant no, we'd be crazy to try any of the rough stuff on them. I looked over at the guys from J.P. One of them had a case of beer out of his car. He was looking very mean. I'd never seen a case of beer at a football game before. I wasn't yet fourteen and I was from Westminster Drive and nobody I knew drank beer on the school grounds.

Marvin Fuchs and Stanley Segal came over. Again Rudnunski said, "They're out to get us," and I knew then what he meant. "Us" meant Jews. Kikes. They didn't want just to win a game, they wanted more than that. They were going to humiliate us even if they had to send us home bleeding.

Marvin Fuchs spoke soothingly to Rudnunski. I couldn't hear what he was saying but it looked like an old rabbi talking to a reluctant Samson. I remember it now as a conversation entirely in Yiddish, but this is probably my own addition to the story. Pinsky came over. He had a bad scrape on his knee, he was aching from being sacked, he was tired from his touchdown run, but he was too furious to be afraid.

"Get your knee into him," said Pinsky. "And if he comes at you from behind, give him the elbow. Like this!" And for Pinsky it was merely a matter of technique. But we all knew, we Jews, that once Rudnunski clobbered Vernon Kiss, Shag Muler and his storm-troopers – Kobluk, Fillion, Bullmer, and all the J.P. zoots – would be on us like an S.S. regiment. If Pinsky knew, he wasn't showing it. Nor was Wiener, our most accomplished fighter. Pinsky and Wiener were talking quietly to the new guy, who I swear had not opened his mouth since he arrived. Up close he was even more thin and pale than before. He looked over at the other sideline at Kiss, Fillion, Bullmer, Kobluk, and Muler, no emotion on his face. Only a trace of stoat-like hunger.

Kobluk kicked off. He tried one of those short bouncers that was supposed to travel only the minimum ten yards so the kicking team could recover it. But Kobluk toed it a bit too hard, and it drifted magnetically into my arms. I hadn't handled the ball once in the entire first half. A buck fever of dread and elation pounding through my system, I charged straight at the horde of oncoming Philistines. The fastest half of our team was well behind me and two slow guys, Marvin and Big Al, were beside me. A ball carrier is supposed to wait long enough to pick up his blocking, but I was too anxious to be a hero and too afraid of being clobbered to think. I got ahead of Big Al and Marvin and cut over to the sidelines and the whole J.P. pack was right on my heels, so I tried to run through a couple of them and someone caught me from behind. But I'd taken the ball into J.P.'s territory, and outside of Pinsky's touchdown run it was the furthest we'd penetrated all game. When I went back to the huddle several guys, Pinsky included, slapped me on the back. That was the last good moment I had in the game.

Pinsky called a short pass to the new guy. Wiener lined up next to me on the left side of the line. We were to draw off some pass defenders by running like hell up the left sideline and Pinsky would just dump it over the line to the new guy.

The ball was snapped and Wiener and I took off and Shag Muler took off with me, but suddenly he stopped. I thought Pinsky must have unloaded to the new guy but I was wrong. Someone was down. I trotted back. Everyone milled around the injured player. It was Rudnunski. He was rolling around on the grass, groaning and swearing.

Vernon Kiss was there commiserating. "Jeez," he said. "Al, I'm sorry." This in a high nasal voice that sounded pretty phony to me. "Are y'all right?"

Al said, "Fuck you, Kiss." It was his thigh, it must have hurt like hell. His groaning came louder.

"What's the matter?" snapped Pinsky.

"Fuckin *kneed* me when I was *down*."

"I never did!"

Vernon Kiss was very tense. Wiener came over, looked him in the eye. "You been kneein Rudnunski since the goddam first quarter, Kiss." Kiss looked stricken because Wiener was very tough. Kiss and I grew up with Wiener. When he was mad he was nothing short of sadistic and right now he was very mad. He was snarling. "You wait till he's *down*, an he can't protect himself, then ya give im the knee!" Wiener was getting his anger up, his fists were clenched, he was almost ready. "Too *chicken* to face him. Ya gotta wait till he's *down*!"

Up stepped Shag Muler, raven-haired, dark-eyed, an axe-blade face jutting forward at Wiener's. "Fuck off, Wiener!"

"Yeah?" said Wiener, but his snarl had suddenly gone off key. He knew he could break Vernon Kiss in two, but he also knew no one could take Shag Muler in a fair fight. Like Kiss, Wiener always avoided fair fights.

"Come on, you guys," said Kobluk. Rudnunski groaned once more. I looked up and Fillion was there too, a bottle of beer in his hand, the long-necked kind. The bottle was empty, and he held it by the neck and tapped his hand nervously with it. His eyes were disturbingly blank. "Come on," said Kobluk, "break it up." He stepped between Muler and Wiener, straddling Rudnunski, who was still holding his leg, swearing and groaning. Never big on brains, Wiener thought he was safe, so he reached past Kobluk and gave Vernon Kiss a shove. Muler leapt over

Rudnunski to face Wiener again. He shoved him hard and Wiener told him: "Go to hell, Muler! Can't Kiss fight his own battles?"

"What'd you say?"

"I said, can't Kiss –"

"The other thing, suckface!"

"I said go to hell," said Wiener quietly. Muler shoved him again.

"Come on, you guys," said Kobluk.

"This is ridiculous," said Fuchs.

But now Muler padded very slowly after Wiener, who suddenly looked much less than the guy who gave Segal a bloody nose the month before, a head shorter than the Wiener who half-drowned one of my old friends in the science room sink. Wiener's voice was practically bawling and Muler hadn't even hit him yet.

"Wiener?" he whispered, soft as a zephyr. "Wiener?" Wiener backed off and Muler kept coming, real slow. "Wiener?"

"What!" bawled Wiener, and Muler spat right in his face, but Wiener wouldn't fight. Muler slapped Wiener's face, but still he wouldn't fight. He grabbed Wiener's arm and twisted and Wiener howled. And then Wiener swung around and belted Muler. He belted him very hard, right in the gut. Muler just stood there. It was a good solid punch and we all knew it, and Muler just smiled. Then belted Wiener full in the face and Wiener started howling. He was an enraged six year old. With sickening dread, we realized that Muler had not finished with him.

I remember that moment like a photograph. Muler was loose, his voice purred, and he was smiling. Kobluk just looked on; Marvin Fuchs looked as though he was witnessing the birth of his blackest prophecies; Big Al, up on one knee now, his own pain momentarily abandoned; Fillion vacant-eyed, no longer tapping his beer bottle on the palm of his hand; Bullmer with that obsessed smile some men wear at ringside; Segal no longer raging but perfectly stoi-

cal, as if awaiting the signal from the leader of a firing-
squad; Wiener howling no more. I remember it in detail
because that's when the new fellow stepped up in front of
Wiener, faced Muler, pointed to his own cock, and to
Muler said, simply, "Bite this." Nobody laughed or moved.
The only sounds were Wiener sniffling, and the October
wind. As many J.P. mouths caught in mid-breath as Jewish mouths, and as if we didn't all hear him the first time,
the new fellow said it again, softly: "Bite this."

He was forgettably drab in his red-straps and white T-
shirt, his oversized socks. He was several inches shorter
than Shag Muler, smaller in every way. And yet quite un-
forgettable. Those prominent cheekbones, slits for eyes,
that thin scruff of hair the colour of dust, that face of a
hungry mink. His hands were down and every boy on the
field, finally, knew why he was here. Muler looked down on
the newcomer, and though his face was as impassive as his
adversary's we knew that Muler would strike first. Shag
Muler. Not cruel like Fillion was reputed to be when
drunk, not mean like Wiener when he bullied smaller
boys, but dangerous when convinced of the rightness of his
cause.

Perhaps he would have relished that first blow more,
aimed it better too, if it had been launched at Wiener. It
was an overhand right and it caught the pale boy hard on
the left ear, but his follow-up left missed, and though the
fellow's ear flushed pink, he moved away, eyes on Muler,
without a flinch of pain, instead summoning Muler to try
again. So Muler slapped him, his admonishment for little
boys who use foul language, and the pale boy came in and
up on him. It was too fast to record, but I remember Muler
clubbing at the dusty head as a gorilla might pound his
own chest and the pale kid, no boxer either but a toe-to-toe
slugger, slashed up at Muler with uppercuts and brawling
overhands, both men landing until something had to give.
Two sounds snapped out of this squawl of arms: one, the
crunch of bone on bone; the other, the wrench of gristle, as

Muler went down, sank slowly to his knees, both hands over his left eye, little rubies of blood seeping between his fingers.

"Hang on! You! Hang on!" said Kobluk needlessly, because the new fellow was just standing there over Muler, as poker-faced as he'd been all afternoon; Fillion, drunk, wasn't moving; or Vernon Kiss, whose mouth was still open; or Wiener, who'd forgotten his own hurt; or Segal, at a loss for words for the first time I'd ever known; or Pinsky, who reminded me oddly of Frankenstein beholding his monster. Then Kobluk went down on his knees and held Muler's head for a better look and Marvin Fuchs handed Kobluk his handkerchief, saw Vernon Kiss's baleful stare, withdrew. "Goddam butted me," mumbled Muler. I approached Rudnunski, Fuchs and I helped him to his feet, and now it's me Vernon Kiss glares at: I am the Jew he's hated for years.

"C'mon, you guys," Pinsky said eventually. We headed for our bikes. As I climbed on mine, still surrounded by my allies mounting theirs, I noticed that our nameless champion was gone.

• • •

I might not have remembered it all in such detail except for what happened today. I was sitting in a bus on Jasper Avenue, cursing my Honda for losing its muffler at precisely the most inconvenient time. Already I could hear my wife Rachel kvetching. When *your* parents used to come for supper we were *always* on schedule, but when mine come all the way from California, you couldn't make supper on time if you had a day's head start.

My goy parents used to profess so stridently to have accepted Rachel that we both knew they hadn't. I would get nervous before those occasions, come home early, fuss with the food and our toddlers, and generally get in Rachel's way. My parents are gone now. But when Shim and

Ebie come up from L.A. it's all sweetness and light. I mean I really *do* love them.

Anyway, while I stew about this, I'm reading an article in today's paper (the one I write for) about a group of hatemongers who plan to set up a colony somewhere in Central Alberta. And suddenly, Alvin Pinsky sits right down beside me. He doesn't recognize me. It's been twenty years at least since I've even seen the guy. He is taller, almost average height, still thin, though he's filled out some. His jacket and trousers are beige, summer weight. Everything about him is cool. Yet there is that same coiled fierceness, that same impatience as he waits for the bus to leave the curb. It's easy to imagine him on his way back to the huddle, a new scrimmage mapping itself like hope or war in his head. I half expect him to spit on his hands for traction. Before he recognizes me I say, "Pinsky, *pass*, for God's sake. I was in the clear."

He turns and gives me a look that is many things: flight, circumspection, shrewd appraisal, annoyance. I am the pursuer, the hotshot's next client, the wise guy perhaps. "Drew? . . . Edmond!"

He still has a brushcut, or perhaps he has returned to one, so I know he won't go for the thumbs like the old radicals do. We shake hands warmly. I suspect, from his perusal, that he notices the paunch I've acquired, the lines of worry. Perhaps in my eyes he sees just a semitone of envy: he is a man now, five foot seven or eight, still athletic, a jogger perhaps. At any rate no longer the runt. I make a little joke about what success has done to my mid-section and he counters with something about how lack of success has kept him lean. His voice is still raspy, hoarse. He sells real estate, claims to have "Little Jerusalem in the bag," by which he means our old neighbourhood. He's working on his second marriage and has two kids. He had a problem with the bottle but claims he gave it up for chain-smoking. Then he tells me, switching subjects as fast as a quarterback with a broken play: "Guess what. Muler, remember him?"

"Who wouldn't?"

"He's tits up."

"Shag Muler's dead?"

"It was in Saturday's paper. Found dead in his own bedroom. I phoned Hrynchuk about it."

"Artie?"

"Right. He kept in touch with Shag. Apparently he had his own construction company. Had it made, for God's sake."

"How did –"

"Bang," says Pinsky, index finger to his temple. "Hrynchuk told me he had a drinking problem, didn't get on with his wife. Mixed marriage."

"Ouch," I said.

"What?"

"That hits home. My wife's Jewish."

"Sheesh," says Pinsky.

"Did Shag Muler marry a Jewish girl too?"

"Muler *was* Jewish."

"*What?*"

"Hardly anyone knew. Muler kept it quiet. In his neighbourhood . . . you know? Very tough neighbourhood."

"I always saw him as a kind of Doberman for the S.S. boys."

"Sure," says Pinsky.

"At least that's how I saw him when *I* was Jewish."

We both laugh. Then I remember another warrior. I have to ask Pinsky, after all those years. "That other kid," I say, "the one who took Muler on, remember?"

"The one who cut him up with the head butt?"

"Yeah. Who was he?" I'd forgotten about the head butt, but I remember asking almost everyone on the team about the strange warrior who beat Muler. Segal, Rudnunski, Fuchs, every one of them gave me the same answer: Pinsky's not saying. I remember asking Rudnunski a year or two later when we were in high school. And he still said, Pinsky's not saying. I heard theories, mind you, but no one could agree on the boy's name or where he came from.

"You never found out?" says Pinsky.

"How could I? It was the best-guarded secret on the street."

"You probably saw his picture in the papers up to about fifteen years ago. Name's Redl, Willie Redl."

"The boxer?"

"Yeah. He was from the East End back then. Friend of mine knew him from boxing at the y." Pinsky grins his old shrewd grin. "He was our protection."

Willie Redl. My God, I had been asked by my paper to write his obit for the sport's page. He'd been the Canadian middleweight champion. Willie had even been managed for a while by Butch Bullmer, whom I'd known as a boy. Then Willie went to New York in the early sixties. They say he was ranked for a while in the top ten. But the years multiplied like the scar tissue on his face, and before he died in the East Jasper Hotel, he had the physiognomy of a Neanderthal with the Pox. Our protection. Who art in earth. Cauliflowered be thy ears.

I say to Pinsky, "That feels like a previous century."

"Ah," he says, only half-listening, "it's a brand new era." He says this like a proud member of the Chamber of Commerce. A brand new era.

Doesn't he see the headline in front of me? SURVIVALISTS SET UP SHOP IN ALBERTA. Pity the non-Aryan who wanders too near their fencelines. Protection becomes infection, hatred dons a bright new mask. *We have come to this ranch to study our scriptures and our weapons*, says the redneck in the caption photo.

The bus rolls to a stop. "See ya," says Pinsky. He hops off and strides down twenty-fourth. That surprisingly long stride. Except it's no longer the walk of a small boy compensating for his size. It's the walk of a man who has places to go, things to do.

This meeting will make for lively talk around the supper table. My Years as a Jewish Athlete. I will hide the newspaper. Shim and Ebie will return to California with their illusions about Canada intact. They will think that hate literature is an American industry. They are so old and small, especially Rachel's dad. Each year he seems to shrink and bend a bit more. Her parents bring out the parent in me. I get protective around them.

And sometimes I cringe at the things we used to say as kids, the racist jokes. If I tell that to Rachel, she'll resurrect her old suspicion that I married her out of some vague sense of guilt. Guilt, for God's sake. I don't think I've ever quite convinced her that she is the great buffer between myself and despair.

I won't even talk about the schoolyard skirmish. And if Rachel asks me where the paper got to tonight, I will lie. *Paper? What paper? Let's go to bed.* Shim and Ebie will be exhausted. Rachel and I will tiptoe up the stairs. All night long we will cover each other like blankets and in the morning it will be a brand new era.

Acknowledgments

Some of these stories appeared previously: "Protection" in *Saturday Night* and *Appearances* (New York); "Getting the Word" in *Fiddlehead* and *Cracked Wheat* (Coteau Books, Regina); "God's Bedfellows" in *Saturday Night* and *More Saskatchewan Gold* (Coteau Books, Regina); "The Father's Love" in *Canadian Literary Review* and *The Old Dance* (Coteau Books, Regina). Part II of "The Elevator" and "This World" were read on CBC Regina. These stories appear here in somewhat revised form.

*

Writing is by no means a team sport, but beginning writers usually need a lot of help: readers, editors, teachers, typists, bartenders, anyone who will listen to them. I was certainly no exception to this rule when I began the first of these stories in 1976. To those who were there when I needed you, I'd like to say thanks. High on the list are Robert Kroetsch and Jack Hodgins, both of them relentless

216   *David Carpenter*

in their criticisms but never stingy with praise. Thanks
also to the Saskatchewan Arts Board for funding; to the
Saskatchewan Writers/Artists' Colony Committee for those
perfect retreats; to their guest editors Vanderhaeghe and
Lane; to the editors, retreatants, and luminaries at the
Banff Centre (*circa* 1984), especially Adele Wiseman and
Don Coles; to Sharon and Peggy for typing; to my editor
Ellen Seligman, who is wise and patient; to my writers
group in town; to my department heads at work, who no
longer send me to Texas; to Linda Reutter, who once performed a rescue; to Willy and Freda (née Ahenakew), who
tried their best to keep me honest; to Anne Szumigalski,
who seems to have known my characters in another life;
and to Kever, who is really something else.

David Carpenter
Saskatoon
October 1987